Winters Day

DM WOLFENDEN

Published by DM Wolfenden January 2017
Copyright © 2016 DM Wolfenden All rights reserved.

ISBN-13: 978-1541184633
ISBN-10: 1541184637

DEDICATION

To everyone who believed in me. Thank you!

DM Wolfenden asserts the moral right to be identified as the author of this work.

This novel is entirely a work of fiction. The names, characters and incidents portrayed in it are the work of the author's imagination. Any resemblance to actual persons, living or dead, events or localities is entirely coincidental.

All rights reserved. No part of this publication may be reproduced, distributed, or transmitted in any form or by any means, including photocopying, recording, or other electronic or mechanical methods, without the prior written permission of the publisher, except in the case of brief quotations embodied in critical reviews and certain other non-commercial uses permitted by copyright law.

This book is sold subject to the condition that it shall not, by way of trade or otherwise, be lent, re-sold, hired out or otherwise circulated without the publisher's prior consent in any form of binding or cover other than that in which it is published and without a similar condition being imposed on the subsequent purchaser.

Other works by DM Wolfenden

Behind Blue Eyes – A vampire horror. Available in ebook and print. Honourable mention 2015 from readers favourite.

Carly – A Novelette available in ebook. The CLUE Awards for Thriller/Suspense Novels 2016 Finalist, winners to be announced in 2017

The Box – A Novelette available in ebook.

Bernie and the beast – A short story available in ebook.

Double trouble, available in print and ebook is a collection of flash fiction, dark poetry and includes DM's short stories, Bernie and the beast, Carly and The Box.

CONTENTS

CHAPTER 1	Jolie	Page 3
CHAPTER 2	Lost Love	Page 24
CHAPTER 3	Peter	Page 40
CHAPTER 4	Alec	Page 48
CHAPTER 5	Decorating	Page 55
CHAPTER 6	Uncle Mike	Page 70
CHAPTER 7	Internet Dating	Page 77
CHAPTER 8	Memories	Page 99
CHAPTER 9	Overdressed	Page 111
CHAPTER 10	Blind Date	Page 125
CHAPTER 11	Old School Friend	Page 143
CHAPTER 12	The Lump	Page 167
CHAPTER 13	Desperation	Page 179
CHAPTER 14	Mistake	Page 192
CHAPTER 15	Burn Baby Burn	Page 211
CHAPTER 16	The Fool	Page 237
CHAPTER 17	Spencer	Page 253
CHAPTER 18	Worried	Page 263
CHAPTER 19	Parole	Page 273

ACKNOWLEDGMENTS

I'd like to thank everyone that has helped me on my little adventure, from my beta readers, editor and proof reader. Your input was invaluable ladies. Most of all, I would like to thank you, the reader. Without you, people like me would not exist

CHAPTER 1 JOLIE

Upbeat Punjabi music played in the background of the restaurant, while the smell of ginger, garlic, cardamom, and onions gave the air a spicy, sweet tang.

Jolie Winters adjusted the belt on her skinny jeans. "I think I'm going to burst."

"Me, too, and we haven't had the cake yet," her cousin Debbie said. Red hair cascaded down her shoulders and over the fluttering sleeves of her leaf-green dress.

Jolie looked Debbie up and down. Her slender frame made her look great in anything. "Maybe I'll go on a diet."

"Don't be so ridiculous. I wish I could put a little more weight on." Debbie clamped her hand on her right breast and wiggled it up and down. "It would have saved me five grand on these bad boys."

"That's what all skinny girls say." *I can eat as much as I want, and never put on weight.* She rolled her eyes at the thought. "I *look* at a piece of cake, and put on two pounds."

"You girls are never happy." Aunt May held up a glass of white wine, and in a thick Scottish accent, said, "Happy birthday, Connie."

Debbie picked up her glass. "Aunt Connie."

Jolie raised her glass. "Happy birthday, Mum. I miss you every day."

May wrapped her hand over Jolie's, and looked at her with so much love and sadness, Jolie had to swallow a lump in her throat. "We all miss her." She gave Jolie's hand a gentle squeeze. "I mind the day we found out yer maw was pregnant."

Debbie whispered in Jolie's ear, "Every year, the same story."

Jolie elbowed Debbie. "And every year, I like to hear it."

May tutted at her daughter.

Debbie brushed a loose curl behind her ear, and stared down at the table. "Sorry."

"Yer Uncle Mike had just told yer grandmother I was pregnant. How that woman hated me. She huffed and tutted, and chewed on her gums, then complained we'd only been married a few weeks, and folk might think we'd had to get married, that I was already with child beforehand. The shame of it all." She glanced from Debbie to Jolie. "I know she was your grandmother, but she always reminded me of a bulldog chewing a wasp. Anyway, Connie was peely waly an' nae her usual bubbly self. Even Mike said she looked ill. She would normally have been bouncing around, like she had ants in her pants."

May tapped Jolie's hand, and continued, "When yer grandma took Mike into the kitchen to tell him how bad I was, and ask if I had trapped him into marriage, I asked yer maw what was wrong. She confided in me she was pregnant, too. Now, I was scared at nineteen, but yer maw was only sixteen, and unmarried. We didn't even know she had a boyfriend. She was terrified to tell the old… sorry, yer grandmother, scared stiff she would make her get rid of the bairn, or throw her out on the street. I wrapped her in my arms, and promised her everything was going to be okay. And she told me, nae matter what, she was keeping the bairn. She already loved you so much."

Jolie smiled, she felt the build-up of tears, and she could see her mother's gentle face in her mind.

May continued, "I grabbed her hand, and marched her into the kitchen. Your grandmother looked at me, as if I was a bad smell brought in on the bottom of someone's shoe. Which, of course, I ignored, and scowled at Mike. Yer maw's hand trembled in mine. I said, 'Mike, we need to take care of Connie. She's having a bairn as well.' Your grandmother surprised us all. She ran to yer maw, and hugged her, crying about her poor bairn, how she would look after her. She loved yer mother — we all did. It was Mike who had shouted the odds, demanding to know who had done this to his wee sister."

Jolie tried not to think about her eighth birthday. The sinking feeling, which always accompanied her, sprang to life. This was a celebration—her mother's birthday. She wouldn't allow darkness to invade her mind. Not tonight.

"Why didn't she ever tell you who my dad was? Did you have any suspicions? Any clues?" Jolie already knew the answer, but couldn't stop herself from asking anyway.

May bowed her head, her breathing quickened. "We've been over this so many times." She put her hand over her mouth. "I would tell ye, if I knew."

Jolie sighed. "I'm sorry; I know this makes you uncomfortable."

"I do know she loved him. But, she loved her little girl more."

Jolie blinked rapidly, afraid the tears would fall.

Debbie held her glass up again. "To family."

"To family," May said.

Jolie clinked her glass on May's, then Debbie's. "To my family. I love you guys."

The crow's feet around May's eyes deepened when she

smiled. "Ye will always be like a daughter to me."

"You're going to make me cry," Debbie said, and bumped shoulders with Jolie. "We should go and really celebrate, paint the town red."

May banged her hand down on the table. "What is wrong with you?" Debbie flushed, as May continued, "Ye know this is hard for Jolie. Well, for all of us…"

Jolie gave a nervous laugh, and tried to hide the grief she still felt. "I'm okay. Let's talk about something else."

"Mum, tell Jolie about the cruise you booked."

Jolie turned from Debbie to her aunt.

May was still throwing daggers at Debbie. "Yer no' want to do that."

"What's going on?" She raised an eyebrow.

"Exactly. That's what I want to know. Who goes on a cruise on their own?"

"I won't be on my own," May said. "Well, yes, I'll be on my own, but it's no' like I will be completely on my own; there are a lot of single folk on the cruise."

Debbie slammed her glass down. "You're not single."

"I never said I was. Yer father isn't around, so I can't go on a couples' cruise."

Jolie's face reddened.

May glanced at Jolie, and ran her fingers through her greying hair. "This is nothing to do with you, honey. Nae one blames you." She turned back to Debbie. "Now look what you've done!"

Debbie pouted.

"There was a good deal on ten days cruising around the Mediterranean. Meeting other folk, who are on their own, is not a crime."

Jolie bit the inside of her mouth. "Please stop fighting. You two are the only family I have. Let's not fight, not tonight, please."

May stood up. Her floral swing dress hugged her tall figure in all the right places, as she walked around to the girls, and put an arm on each of their shoulders. "I love you both, so much. But, yer have a bevvy in you, yer both pains in the arse."

"Hey!" Debbie shouted.

"I've only had one drink," Jolie protested.

May laughed. "I'm nae going to do anything to hurt yer dad, Debbie. Now, I'm going home for a nice cup of tea. You two have fun."

They said their goodbyes. Debbie topped up their glasses with wine, and said, "Now Mum's gone, we can finish the bottle, and go have some real fun."

Jolie groaned, and slapped her forehead with her palm. "What have I gotten myself into?"

The girls walked out of the restaurant, and turned when the door of the bar next door slammed. Suddenly, a man stumbled in front of them, and fell to the ground. He was drenched in sweat, and the yellow street lights gave the white-haired man's face an eerie glow. Jolie rushed to him. The stench of stale sweat and beer caused her to flinch and screw up her nose. She turned her head, and took a deep breath before acknowledging him. "Are you hurt, do you need help?"

The man swatted her away, as he stood up. He stumbled backwards; Jolie grabbed his arm to steady him.

His wild, hooded eyes stared at her. "They were chasing me—the demons. They can't catch old Bernie." He patted her hand, before he pulled out of her grip. "Be careful, Miss," he whispered. "They likes pretty girls." His eyes narrowed, as he leaned towards Jolie. "I know you." He jerked back. "Got to stay away." He hit himself on the side of the head repeatedly.

Goosebumps rose up on Jolie's arms, and she

shuddered.

Bernie grimaced a toothless smile, and staggered down the street.

Debbie looked toward the pub doorway. "Poor old boy, ninety-nine pence short of a pound." She shrugged. "Let's get a drink."

Jolie stepped back. She rubbed her arms, and stared at the sign. The Devil's Ride. "From the pub with the demons in it, that've been chasing Bernie?"

"That stuff really gets to you, doesn't it? You read too many ghost stories." Debbie laughed. "You're a complete idiot at times."

Jolie pouted. "I'm not a *complete* idiot; some parts of me are missing."

Debbie flung her arm over Jolie's shoulder. "And that's what I love about you. You're crazy and a right old scaredy pants."

"I love you, too. So much that if we were on a sinking ship together, and there was only one life jacket... I'd really miss you." They laughed at the old joke.

The fading dark blue wallpaper, along with the beer-stained, burgundy velvet chairs and grimy tables, gave the room a depressing tone. The beat of loud dance music pulsated throughout her body. Everyone seemed to avoid the walls. The dozens of patrons gathered in the middle of the floor and around the bar area. She wrinkled her nose, the faint smell of stale smoke and beer assaulting her senses.

The two women squeezed through the revellers to order their drinks.

Jolie leaned on the bar, and her arm landed in a pool of something cold. She sniffed. Beer. She scowled, as she took a tissue out of her brown leather handbag, and wiped at the liquid.

"Hi," the barman said, and licked his lips. "What can I get you, gorgeous?"

"Two vodka and diet cokes, please."

The barman bent forward, and put his hand near his ear, his eyes focused on her chest. "What was that, sexy?"

Sleazebag. She thrust two fingers in the air, and shouted over the music. "Two vodka and diet cokes."

He nodded, and turned away.

Jolie picked up the drinks, and cringed when she caught sight of herself, and the little jagged white lines across her face in the mirror, which ran the full length of the bar. After all these years, they still made her feel sick. Reminded her that her mother had died the night she got them.

Debbie twirled her hair around her index finger, as Jolie handed her the drink.

Jolie held the glass up to her lips and sipped, taking in the crowd of revellers, laughing and joking, and trying to have conversations over the thumping beat. "Let's go to the back. I can hardly hear myself think."

"What?" Debbie asked, she dipped her finger in the glass and slowly popped it in her mouth, as her gaze wandered around the crowd.

Jolie jerked her head to the side, and traversed her way through the crowd, across the floor. "Excuse me," she said, and slid between two young men. A hand cupped her backside. She glared at the spotty teenager. "Arsehole."

Debbie nudged her. "Did he just grab your bum?"

"Yeah, he looks about fourteen years old." She sighed. "Why would you want to come in here?"

"Stop moaning. A few more vodkas, and you'll be enjoying yourself. Besides, you get plenty of talent in here."

"And where do you see all this talent?" Jolie laughed.

Debbie pointed. "How about him?"

"Who?" Jolie scanned the room.

"Him." Debbie pointed again towards a young man with long dark hair, in a white t-shirt.

Jolie shook her head. "For goodness sake, he's wearing more hair products than me. He does have a cute bum, but we haven't seen his face yet."

Debbie eyed him demurely when he turned and faced her. "He just looked at us, and smiled."

Jolie bit her bottom lip as her gaze went from his broad shoulders down to his trim waist. "He *does* have a gorgeous body."

"He's coming over." Debbie popped a button on Jolie's plain cream blouse.

"What the hell?" Jolie went to refasten her blouse; Debbie swatted her hand out of the way.

"If you've got it, flaunt it. There's no shame." Debbie winked, and tugged her dress down, wiggled, and pushed her boobs up with the palms of her hands.

Jolie felt the heat rise in her face. "I thought we were just having a quick drink?"

Debbie didn't reply, her eyes fixed on her prey.

Jolie tapped her on the shoulder. "I'm going to the toilet, and then, I'm going to get a taxi." Her brow furrowed, as she glanced at her open blouse. She grabbed the button. When she turned to walk away, the man stood in front of her.

"Hello." He smiled. "Do you believe in love at first sight, or should I walk by again?"

Jolie's face was on fire, as she fumbled with one hand to refasten her shirt.

"Do you need a hand with that?" he asked.

The button slipped into place, and Jolie downed her

drink in one gulp. "Look, buddy, I have a boyfriend."

He leered at her chest. "And I have a pet grasshopper."

She leaned away from him. "What?" She squinted, and searched his large grey eyes for clues of substance abuse.

"I thought we were talking about things that do not matter." His smile made his eyes twinkle.

Jolie stood straight, squared her shoulders, and looked him up and down. "I will always cherish the initial misconceptions I had about you." She turned away from him, and glared at Debbie, who was bent over laughing.

"What does that mean?" he asked, his hands out to the side.

"Ignore her, she's weird. I'm Debbie." She held out her hand.

He took her hand in his, bent over, and kissed the back of it.

"Such a gentleman," Debbie gushed.

"Alec."

Jolie huffed.

"If you want to go to the bar and get a couple of Vodka and Cokes, Alec, we could have fun tonight." Debbie fluttered her long dark lashes at him.

Alec almost ran to the bar.

Jolie put her hand on her hip and glared at her. "What are you doing?"

"If you don't want him, I'll ride him like a bull. And that accent of his is, like, really posh."

"He's only after a one-night stand, and that's not me. He's not interested in getting to know me. He just wants sex. I can't blame him. Nobody wants the Bride of Frankenstein on their arm."

Debbie's face creased. "Stop it. Stop feeling sorry for

yourself. So, you have a few, barely-noticeable scars on that gorgeous face of yours." She pulled her shoulders back and stuck her chest out, as the guy returned with the drinks.

Jolie excused herself, and went to the bathroom. She took two painkillers out of her bag, popped them in her mouth, and rubbed her temples with her fingers. The throbbing pain on the left side of her head had started to make her vision blurry.

Debbie and the guy were kissing passionately when Jolie returned. Debbie spotted her, and laughed. The sounds in the pub echoed around Jolie's head like a wailing banshee.

Jolie tugged Debbie towards her. "If you are going to be all over this guy, like a bad smell — a guy whose name you don't even know, I might add, then I'm off home. It's a bad enough day, as it is. I'm not playing gooseberry, sitting in the middle of you two making out."

Debbie's eyes widened. "I'm so sorry."

Jolie shook her head. "It's okay. I'm just feeling a bit low, and my head is pounding." She cupped Debbie's face. "You have fun, I'm going home."

Debbie grabbed her in a bear hug. "I'll come with you."

Jolie prised herself out of Debbie's arms. "I can't breathe! For someone so skinny, you have a grip like an oversized American wrestler." She paused. "And don't be daft. You have fun, and call me tomorrow."

Debbie grinned, showing off her pearly white teeth. "Thanks. I was hoping you wouldn't mind. I'm on a promise with the studmuffin."

Jolie crossed her arms over her chest. "The studmuffin?"

"Yep, I had a quick feel, and he won't disappoint. If

you know what I mean." Debbie wiggled her eyebrows up and down.

"You're a complete hussy." Jolie laughed. She uncrossed her arms, and kissed Debbie's cheek before leaving.

The amber street lighting gave the dark shop windows an eerie glow, as she crossed the street to the almost deserted taxi rank. A man stood in the shadows, the end of his cigarette lit up like a beacon in the dark. She gripped her handbag and held it close to her body.

"Jolie."

She froze; a cold shiver ran down her spine. "Dave."

He dropped the cig on the ground and stood on it, before he sauntered over to her, with his hands in the pockets of his suit pants, a cheesy grin on his face. "God, you look great. It's been ages."

The pounding in her head seemed to intensify. Her throat dried up, and she closed her eyes.

"Jo, I'm sorry…"

Her eyes sprung open, and glared at him. "Don't call me Jo. Just leave me alone."

A taxi pulled up.

"This last year…"

Jolie kept her clenched fists close to her body, and cut him off. "You were here first."

Dave sighed. "No, you take it."

"Thanks," she sneered.

He grabbed her sleeve, as she opened the car door. She yanked her arm away. "Don't touch me!"

He held out a small white card. "Can we talk, sometime? Please."

Jolie glared at him from the corner of her eye. Her nails scraped the back of his fingers when she snatched the card from his. She slid inside the taxi and slammed the door, the screwed-up card still in her shaking hand.

She wanted to talk to Debbie, but she was busy, so she called her old school friend, Molly. "Hey Molly, it's Jolie."

"Hiya, thought you were out with Debbie and her mum?"

Jolie sighed. "She has copped off, with some posh bloke called Alec."

"Are you okay? You sound upset?"

Jolie bit her bottom lip. "Yeah…no. I just saw Dave." The phone stayed silent for a few moments. "Why can't I be happy? All I ever wanted was to get married and have a family. And he ruined that."

"You can't let him ruin the rest of your life. You need to get out there, and meet someone new."

Jolie giggled. "You sound just like Debbie."

"Watch it."

Both girls laughed.

Jolie looked at the card in her hand. "Debbie still wants me to try the online dating thing."

"Would it really be so bad?" Molly asked.

"I don't know. The thought of it scares me a little."

"Everyone meets people on the net these days. As long as you take precautions…"

Jolie cut her off. She had the same conversation over and over with her cousin, and didn't want to get into it with her friend. "I'm nearly home. I'm going to go straight to bed. I'll phone you tomorrow." And she ended the call.

CHAPTER 2 Lost Love

For the past week, all of Jolie's dreams seemed to be about her ex-boyfriend. Last night's was the worst.

Dave waved at her in the distance.

She ran towards him, but he kept getting further and further away. "Wait," she called out.

He lay in bed next to her, his naked chest glistened with sweat. He turned away from her.

"I love you," he said.

She leaned over him, and another woman lay in his arms.

She pounded her fists off his back, as their laughter got louder and louder.

When she woke up, it took a minute to realise it had just been a dream; he wasn't next to her. She shook off the feelings of disappointment, hurt, and longing.

Jolie sighed. Bright red numbers insulted her, and she let out a groan. 04:02. There was no way she would get back to sleep.

She threw off the lavender quilt and rolled out of bed. As she stumbled to the bathroom, she bumped her right shoulder on the door frame, and only just managed to avoid hitting her face. "Son-of-a…"

Purposely sidestepping the large mirror on the wall, she entered the bathroom. She didn't like looking into mirrors at the best of times, but on five hours' sleep? Not a chance in hell.

The pressure of the water prickled her face. In her mind, she pictured Dave embracing the other woman, his strong arms wrapped around her tiny waist, her long blonde hair whipping around in the wind. She slid down the tiled wall, and sobbed into her hands.

The gentle heat warmed her muscles, and eventually, she relaxed. The noise of the water helped clear her mind.

Half an hour later, Jolie stood in the doorway of the living room, towel wrapped around her head. She tied her bath robe. Everything reminded her of Dave. The fifty-inch television used to play his games; she had complained it was too big the day he'd bought it. The brown leather four-seater couch where they had cuddled; sometimes, they'd fallen asleep there until morning, locked in each other's arms. The white sheepskin rug they'd made love on the day they had bought it.

She opened a drawer in the ebony dresser, and took out her photo album. Jolie hadn't looked at the album since the relationship ended. She flipped it open to a random page – a picture of them at the boardwalk. Dave's deep blue eyes and his cheeky smile almost caused a physical pain. That smile had melted her heart on many occasions. Ice cream dripped down his fingers. She could almost hear the seagulls squawking, as one pinched his ice-cream. She had captured the moment perfectly; along with his flawless smile.

It was his smile she'd fallen for at school. They had both been fourteen. Dave kicked a football, and it hit her between the shoulder blades. He ran over apologising, and when their eyes had met, he smiled. It had made her go weak at the knees.

"Cool scars. They make you look like a bad arse," he'd said. "Want to hang out later?" And they'd hung out from that day on.

She put the album down, and walked over to her handbag. Her hand trembled, as she struggled to slide the zipper open. Holding her breath, she reached inside and withdrew the crumpled card—and her phone.

Then, a glint of shiny orange and silver across the room caught her attention. Jolie move over to her fish tank, and rubbed the glass with her finger, watching her goldfish dart back and forth. "Good morning, Spencer. I've not forgotten about you," she said, as she lifted the hardback book off the top of tank's lid. She slid the cover back a few inches. "What do you fancy for breakfast, pellets or flakes?" She picked up a small plastic tub and unscrewed the lid. "Whoa." She pulled a face, as the smell of dried fish assaulted her nostrils. "Yummy. Flakes it is. I'll get you some brine shrimps later."

Jolie pinched a few flakes between her fingers, and dipped them in the tank's water a couple of times. The fish swam up, and tried sucking on her fingers. "Spencer, they have to soak a little, or you'll get sick." She stroked the dorsal fin with her other hand. "You're the only man in my life, you know that? And you're a fish," she said sadly, and released the flakes into the water.

Jolie remembered the day Dave had won Spencer at the fair.

They walked past the fairground stall. "Three hoops for a pound. Get the hoop over any prize to win," the grimy man said.

"That fish looks so sad," Jolie said.

Dave's shoulders shook with laughter. "It's a fish. How can you tell?"

Jolie never took her eyes off the fish. It, too, stayed perfectly still, watching her.

Dave glanced from the fish to Jolie. "Whoa. That's creepy. All the other fish are swimming about."

"Excuse me, how much for the fish?" she asked.

The man popped the cigarette in his mouth, the end a yellowy red when he inhaled. Blue grey smoke escaped as he spoke. "Three hoops for a quid."

She held out a pound coin. "What about the bowl?"

"A fiver," he replied with a sneer. He counted out the dirty, dull red and blue-coloured rubber rings and put them down on the wooden ledge around the edge of the stall.

Her hand trembled.

Dave put his hand on top of hers. "I'll do it. I got this." He winked, picked up the ring, and focussed on his target. It flew up in the air, hit the edge of the bowl, and spun around and around, then effortlessly wound its way down.

Jolie jumped up and threw her arms around his neck, knocking him backwards a step. "Thank you. I knew there was a reason I loved you."

"Because of my ability to rescue fish? And to think, all this time I thought it was my body," he said, and slid his hands around her waist.

The phone beeped and brought Jolie back to the present. It was a text from Debbie.

I've not seen you all week, you OK?

Yeah, I'm going to Aunt May's later. See you there? Jolie replied.

Sure. Pick me up?

OK.

***

Jolie followed Debbie into the brightly lit living area of Aunt May's house. She ran her fingers over the burgundy, Chesterfield suite. A cool breeze ruffled the curtains at the open window, stirring up the sweet smell of baked apples and cinnamon, and reminding her of home.

"Mum," Debbie called out.

"I'm in the kitchen."

The kitchen counter was littered with sugar, flour, and apple skins. Three pies stood on a cooling tray, steam drifting in the air.

May slid an uncooked pie inside the oven.

"Wow, how many are you making, Mum?"

May swung round, the creases on her flour covered face deepened with her smile. "You can both take one home." She wiped her hands on her apron. "Give me a minute to clean this mess up. Are ye hungry?"

Both girls said, "No."

Jolie picked the kettle up. "I'll make a brew."

"Yer an angel, I'd love a cuppa." May handed Debbie the apple skins. "Fling them out back for the birds, love."

Jolie poured the hot water into the teapot, placed it on the tray, and took it over to the round dining table.

Her stomach turned over, as she stared at the tired, Melamine cabinets, mismatched chairs, and chipped counter tops. It had all looked so shiny and new when she'd arrived here fifteen years ago. She had sat at this table, picking at the lace doilies, wondering when she could go home, when her mother would be released from hospital, and why Uncle Mike wasn't here. Little did she know, her mother would never come home again, and Uncle Mike would be sentenced to twenty years in prison. Eight-year-old Debbie had joined her at the table, and handed her a piece of liquorice. "Do you want to come to my room and play with my toys?" she'd asked.

May rubbed Jolie's arm. "You okay, sweetheart?"

Jolie snapped back into the present, and nodded before sitting down. "I was thinking about the doilies that used to be on the table."

May laughed. "Those horrible lace things your grandmother gave us, god rest her soul. I got rid of those years ago." May picked the teapot up and started pouring the drinks.

"Apart from them, it's just the same. The kitchen, I mean."

May poured the milk into the cup and handed it to Jolie. "Old and tired, just like me."

"You're not old." Jolie put a spoonful of sugar in and stirred.

Suddenly, the back door slammed shut. They both turned and stared at Debbie.

"Slam it a bit louder next time will ye? I don't think they heard it in the next street," May said.

Debbie tutted, and sat down at the table.

May shrugged and passed her a cup. "Pass us that pie will ye, love? We'll have a piece with our tea."

"You could have asked before I sat down."

May held her hands up in surrender. "I'll get it myself."

The chair screeched along the tiled floor when Debbie forced it back. "I've got it."

Jolie burst out laughing. "Honestly, if you two were being watched by a stranger, they would not believe you actually cared for each other. You're like a feuding couple, rather than mother and daughter."

Debbie placed the pie and a knife down on the table. May took hold of her hand and brought it to her lips. "She's my baby."

"I love you, too."

"When are you going on that cruise?" Jolie asked.

Debbie went to open her mouth, but Jolie kicked her foot. "Ouch, what was that for?"

"Play nice."

"Two weeks' time. I'm sure looking forward to seeing all those countries."

"It sounds exciting." Jolie nudged Debbie. "Doesn't it?"

Debbie smiled sarcastically.

"I fly to Spain, and then set sail from Barcelona. From

there, we travel to Mallorca, France, Greece, Croatia, and eventually end up in Rome." May sat back, her face a picture of excitement. "I cannae believe it. Me, in all those places."

"You'll have an amazing time. We'll take you to the airport." Jolie kicked Debbie again.

Debbie hissed, and rubbed her foot. "Sure, we'll see you off."

When the girls left May's house, Jolie had an idea. "What do you say we redecorate the kitchen for your mum while she's away?"

Debbie slipped her arm through Jolie's. "She would love that."

They got in the car, but Jolie stared into space.

Debbie stared at Jolie. "She puts the key in the ignition, turns it, and starts the car."

"Funny, my little *Silence of the Lambs* wannabe. And, it puts the lotion in the basket. Isn't it?"

"Stop being an idiot, or I will be lowering a basket down to you."

Jolie stared down at her hands. "I need to ask you something."

Debbie stayed silent, but Jolie could feel her eyes boring into her.

Keeping her head down, she peeked at Debbie from the corner of her eye. "Do you blame me for your Dad being in prison?"

"We all know you blame yourself." Debbie slid her hand around Jolie's. "But, no one else blames you, just *you*. You were eight years old. Your stepdad was evil, if my dad hadn't of stopped him…" She paused, and took a deep breath. "I don't believe he regrets killing that scum for a second." She lifted Jolie's hand up to her mouth, and placed a gentle kiss on her knuckles. "Philip

Chapman killed your mum, and if Dad hadn't got there, god knows what he would have done to you." She stroked the scars on the left side of Jolie's face. "Smashing a glass in your face was…"

Jolie took a shaky breath, pushed Debbie's hand away from her face, and sniffed.

"I'm sorry, I love you."

Jolie wiped her nose with the back of her hand. "I love you, too."

Red and blue flashing lights and a wailing siren passed them.

A nervous laugh escaped Jolie's mouth. "Isn't it weird how when a cop drives by, you feel paranoid, instead of protected?"

"Well, you better start the car, before they come and arrest you for acting daft."

Jolie blinked away the moisture in her eyes, wiped her face with the back of her hand, and then started the engine.

A little while later, the girls arrived at Jolie's flat. Debbie went in the living room, while Jolie grabbed a couple of beers from the red 1950s American-style Smeg fridge. Then, her face paled. She put the bottles down on the side, and rushed to the fish tank. The lid was slightly ajar, and Spencer flapped around in the open draw. She picked him up, and gently placed him back in his tank. She ran her hand over the book which normally weighted the lid down. It brought back a memory of Spencer the morning after she'd brought him home.

Jolie walked into the living room, and screamed for Dave. Spencer lay on the floor, his golden scales almost completely black. She dropped to her knees, scooped the fish up, and lowered him into his bowl.

Dave ran into the living room. "What's wrong?"

Jolie pointed at the bowl. Spencer was on his side, unmoving. "He was on the floor."

Dave knelt down beside her, kissed the back of her head, and tapped the glass. Spencer jerked, then turned the right way up.

Dave stood up, grabbed a large leather-bound book, and put it on top of the bowl.

Jolie stared in horror. "What if he suffocates?"

Dave peered through glass. "He's not going to run out of air. Come on, it's ten o'clock. Mum's expecting us at eleven."

Jolie pursed her lips. "You're not a fish expert. You can't know for sure."

"For god sake!" He slammed his hand down on the unit, and glared at her. "It's a stupid, bloody fish."

The blood drained from her face. She stared at the floor, her heart pounding in her chest. Willing herself to calm down, she wanted to disappear, to melt into the cracks between the floorboards.

"You'd better get dressed, we're going to be late!"

She flinched, as he yelled.

"Why do you do that? I've never laid a finger on you! Why do you act all scared?" he growled. "I'm not your stepdad."

The muscles in her jaw tensed.

"Get dressed," he ordered.

She peeked up when his footsteps faded. With a shaky breath, she wiped a stray tear from her cheek.

When Jolie and Dave arrived back home, Spencer was on the living room floor again. The fish flapped about, his mouth opening and closing, as he gasped and suffocated. Dave picked him up by the tail, threw him into the bowl, and mumbled something Jolie couldn't make out.

"Be gentle with him, he's sad," Jolie said. She reached for the bowl and ran her finger back and forth on the glass. Spencer moved in time with her movements.

"He's not normal." Dave said, then he laughed. "A bit like you."

"It's not funny." She picked up the bowl. "We'll have to take it in turns watching him tonight."

"What?"

"It's only for one night." She hugged the bowl to her body.

Dave shook his head. "If you think I'm going to be on suicide watch for a bloody demented goldfish, you can think again."

"I'll get him a proper tank tomorrow—and some friends."

Debbie's shouting stirred Jolie from the memory. She gave Spencer one last glance. "But, you killed your little friends, didn't you, Spencer?" Jolie placed the book on top of the lid, and picked up the beer bottles.

Jolie stopped in the living room doorway, and held her breath.

Debbie held up the crumpled card. "What's this?"

She couldn't meet Debbie's eye. "I saw him last week."

Debbie threw her arms up. "What do you mean you *saw* that two timing—"

"I was going for a taxi. I blew him off."

Debbie raised her eyebrows. "Good for you."

"He gave me the card, and asked me to call him."

"You should have rammed it down his throat!"

Jolie flushed. "I just put it in my purse."

"You're not seriously thinking about calling him, are you? Don't you remember the mess you were in when he left?" Debbie shook her head. "You need to get out there, get laid, and get over him."

Jolie's shoulders slumped. "I don't know, maybe. I nearly called him this morning."

"You *what?* Are you serious?"

"But, I didn't. Forget him. How did it go with Alec?"

Debbie gently cupped Jolie's face. "Oh, sweetie, he'd only do it again. A leopard doesn't change its spots."

"I know. Now, tell me about Alec. I can't remember

the last time you went on a second date with anyone."

"Okay, but I know you're just changing the subject to get out of admitting what a shit he is." Debbie grinned, and released Jolie's face. "Alec is amazing. The things he can do with his…"

Jolie put her hands over her ears. "Eww, enough details already. I'm sorry I asked."

Debbie's phone buzzed. She took it out of her pocket, and giggled. "You know that guy I've been talking to online?"

Jolie shrugged. "Which one?"

"Jason." She rechecked her phone. "Jamie."

"Glad to see you've gotten to know him well enough to remember his name."

Debbie poked her tongue out. "It was a momentary lapse. Jason is… never mind about him. Jamie's in town tonight. Guess I won't be catching up on any sleep." She winked at Jolie. "You should try it. Honestly, as long as you take precautions, there's no more danger than meeting someone at work, or in a pub. I can set a profile up for you."

At the all-too familiar suggestion, Jolie's scars throbbed as they did whenever she felt coerced into something. She touched her face with her fingertips, and felt an embarrassing deep flush spread across her face. She didn't need a mirror to tell her that her fair skin had turned as red as beetroot. "Not this again. Anyway, it's not for the likes of me."

"Oh, I'm deeply sorry, Your Highness. Should I go get you your tea and crumpets now?"

Jolie slapped her on the hand. "You know what I mean."

"Yeah, you're too shy, can't talk to men, blah blah blah."

She's right, but I can't do it, not yet. "I told you a hundred times, *no*. I'm ending this conversation now."

CHAPTER 3 PETER

Jolie parked her car behind McCarthy, Richards, and Day - Architects and Surveyors.

The angry grey sky did nothing to lift her mood. Her shoulder banged into the door, as she tried to open it. Confused as to why the door wouldn't open, she checked her watch. Eight twenty-five. *I'm usually the last in.* She peered through the window at the large oval clock above the reception desk. Seven forty-five, what the hell? A rumble of thunder echoed in the distance, and the heavens opened. She groaned, and drew her white wool cardigan across her chest, as the cold dollops of water splashed down on her.

Jolie was about to leave when Harold McCarthy and his secretary of three years, Sophia, pulled up in a taxi. Harold, a small heavyset man in his fifties, with a hooked nose and the worst comb-over she had ever seen, had started the company back in the early nineties. Sophia's slim, shapely legs elegantly glided out of the taxi. She stopped and glared at Jolie. Her bleach blonde hair emphasized her sharp features and thin lips. Jolie guessed her age at forty; though someone did mention it was her thirtieth birthday this year.

"Nice and early I see, Jolie. That's the spirit. Can't remember the last time someone beat me in." Harold's jowls wobbled on his aging face.

"Good morning, Harold." Jolie put on her best

fake smile, then turned to the woman and nodded. "Sophia."

The keys jingled, as Harold pulled them from his overcoat pocket. Jolie tensed; the noise grated through her already hungover brain.

"Rough night?" Sophia replied, with a smirk, and pointed at Jolie's camel-coloured dress.

Jolie looked down, and ran her hand over the front of her dress to straighten out any creases. Her hands touched flesh when she went to straighten the back. She held her breath, closed her eyes, and quickly tugged the bottom of her dress out of her bright yellow and black Batman knickers.

Convinced her cheeks were now a blinding red, she nodded a thanks to Sophia, who was trying, not to laugh directly in her face.

Jolie followed them into the reception area, and flipped the light switch. Bright fluorescent lights buzzed to life. Sophia and Harold entered a door to the left.

Jolie had worked at the office for six years. The place had always given her a feeling of safety. Here, she had control, a schedule, a routine, everything was in its place, and nothing ever changed. She answered the phone, typed up the letters, and opened the post.

Her shoes clip-clopped on the dark wood flooring, as she walked over to the polished slate reception desk. She rubbed her fingers over the uneven texture of the red brick wall, and smiled. Her handbag dropped with a thud on the desk.

When Jolie made her way into the kitchen a few minutes later, Sophia's shrill voice caused her to wince.

"Harold would like a tea, and I'll have a coffee.

Black," she said.

Just like your soul. Jolie shuddered, and mumbled, "A please would be nice."

Jolie felt Sophia's eyes glaring into the back of her skull. "Well, did you hear me?"

Her body tensed. *This is why I don't come in early. I've had enough of your attitude.* She took a deep breath, and glowered over her shoulder. "Manners cost nothing."

Sophia placed her hand on her chest. "What, do you expect me to make *your* coffee?"

Hands on her hips, Jolie faced her. "I'm sick of you thinking you are better than everyone else. I am not your dog's body." Her outburst shocked herself, but this had been building up for years.

Sophia's eyes widened, and she edged back under the glare.

The bell on the main door chimed, when Peter walked in, with another of the firm's young surveyors. He looked from Jolie to Sophia, and back to Jolie. He ran his fingers through his short light brown hair. "What's going on?"

"Nothing, I'm just about to make a cuppa. You two want anything?"

"I'll be in my office," Sophia said.

Jolie balled her fists, and turned away. She filled the kettle to boil water for tea, and switched on the coffee maker. She grabbed a mug from the draining board, and slammed it down.

Peter placed his hand on her shoulder. "You okay?"

Unable to look at him, she nodded, and reached for another cup, slamming that one down, too.

"Don't think the mugs would agree. Anyway, you do know what time it is?"

Jolie faced him, crossing her arms over her chest. "I'm really not in the mood. She winds me up on purpose."

"Ignore the stuck-up cow. I know what will make you feel better." He winked at her. His dark eyes had a glint of amusement in them.

She raised her eyebrow. "Oh really?"

"Mocha latte from the coffee shop." He wiggled his eyebrows up and down.

She couldn't help herself, and giggled. He always managed to lift her mood. "Do you know how much you mean to me, Peter Day?" She cupped his strong jaw in her hands.

He leaned into her hold on him.

"I think I would be up on assault charges by now if it weren't for you."

He placed his hand on top of hers. "Someone has to know your secret deactivation code. It could mean the end of the world otherwise."

The steam from the kettle wafted through the air, like a genie emerging from a lamp. Jolie rubbed her temples with her fingertips, and looked at the coffee machine. She grinned, and reached up for a dust-covered jar on the top shelf.

***

Jolie sat with her hands around the paper coffee cup, when Sophia stormed in, her face like thunder.

Sophia's pointy red nail sliced through the air. "What have you done?" She held the mug up. "What the hell is this crap?"

Julie smirked. "Coffee."

Peter turned his broad shoulders, and asked, "What's the problem now, Sophia?"

Sophia's bottom lip stuck out. "It's her! She's

trying to poison me."

He stood up, and held his hand out for the cup. "I don't think anyone is trying to poison you," he said.

I might, if I got the chance. Jolie put her hand over her mouth to try and hide the grin she couldn't stop forming.

Sophia ran her index finger down Peter's well-toned arm. He took the cup, and raised it to his nose. Her bottom lip trembled. "She hates me. You have no idea what she's really like." She spoke low. "It's like when she brought that fish to work. She knew I was allergic to them. Freaky thing, just like his owner. If she brings it near me again, it's dead"

That's it. Jolie shot up so fast, her chair clattered on the floor. "You threatening my fish? Just because you have some weird fish allergy?"

"See!" Sophia squawked, shielding herself behind him. "She's attacking me again."

"Let's all calm down." Peter turned towards Jolie, his lip twitching with amusement. "What did you do to it?"

"It's not poisoned." Jolie picked up the chair. "It's instant."

Peter burst out laughing.

Sophia huffed and stormed out, her body shuddering, as her high heels slipped on the wood flooring.

"Poor cow, she's never been the same since the house fell on her sister," Jolie said.

Peter chuckled. "You're evil. Be careful the witch doesn't drop a house on you." His eyes held hers for a brief moment, then he blinked. "How's Spencer? Any more great escapes?"

"No. He's on lockdown." *Did I put the book back on*

the lid this morning?

"You should call him, 'Braveheart.'"

She pulled a face. "Very funny."

"Are you coming out tonight?"

"No, could you imagine me and hangover putting up with that? I'd end up killing her."

"I'm meeting an old college roommate." He chuckled. "Probably better you are not in the same vicinity as him. Not sure he's your cup of tea; he's got a sick sense of humour."

"I'm intrigued."

"He would test the patience of a saint, at times." Peter chuckled. "How he ever got a girl at college was unbelievable.

"I missed you when you were at Uni," Jolie suddenly found herself saying. "It felt like someone had taken my rock away. That sounds really selfish, doesn't it? I missed hanging out together, the talks…" She remembered the pain of missing him, how she almost told him she wanted more than friendship, and would have done it, if hadn't been for Dave. *Why couldn't I have found someone like you to fall in love with?*

Peter smiled at her. It was almost as if he was going to speak, but then, changed his mind.

Jolie began to feel self-conscious, and avoided looking at him. "I better get some work done." And she left, taking a deep breath.

CHAPTER 4 ALEC

Jolie ran her hand over her stomach, and sighed. She grabbed the jeans and baggy white shirt off the bed.

She took another look in the mirror, and pinched the tiny bit of flesh overhanging the top of her jeans. "I need to glam this up. Debbie will be stunning, as usual." *The peacock set.*

She padded across the thick beige carpet to her white chest of drawers. Opening the top drawer, she took out her black jewellery box. She took out the silver and rhinestone peacock-shaped chunky choker. The green, turquoise, and blue gems sparkled in the light, as she lifted it up to her slender neck. She took out a matching chandelier earring. Her brow creased, and she shuffled the contents about. "Crap, where's the other one?"

She raked through the drawers in the bedroom, knickers and bras flying through the air.

In the bathroom, she pulled open the top wicker drawer at the side of the white basin. Nothing. She opened the middle drawer, and smiled at the earring glinting in the light. Then, her fingers caught the edge of a photograph also in the drawer. Her hand shook, as she picked up the picture. A tear ran down her right cheek. She screwed the photo up, and launched it at the bin, and screamed out, as the back of her hand caught the edge of the sink.

"Ow. Jesus." She took a deep breath, and shook her hand, placing it close to her chest. She grimaced, as pain ran up her arm. *Shit, this is going to bruise. Ice.*

She made her way to the kitchen, and took out a bag of frozen peas. She flinched when it touched her swollen knuckles.

Her mobile phone rang. She winced, as she grabbed the phone. "Hi, Debbie, I know I'm running late. I'll be there in fifteen minutes."

"Alec's dying to meet you properly."

Jolie giggled. "Now I know he's crazy, dating you and wanting to meet me. Ciao." She put the phone in her bag, threw the peas in the bin, and looked down at her hand. The bruising already began to show. "Great."

***

Jolie sat down at the rickety table, and ran a cleansing wipe over the dirty surface, as she glanced around at the clientele. A group of women in their twenties sat, with their heads close together, trout-pouts on, taking selfies. A gang of middle-aged men jumped up and roared, when they saw their team score a goal on the overhead TV. She looked to the opposite side of the room, and cringed at a bearded and white-haired middle-aged man pawing at a young woman.

She shuddered, and turned to Debbie. "Where is Mr. Misconception, then?"

Debbie pulled a face at her. "Don't call him that. He's not the brightest, and big words confuse him. You'll like him. He's so funny."

"I've experienced it. He had a pet grasshopper." She sensed someone standing behind her, and turned around.

His grey eyes twinkled, just like the first time she saw him. He put the glasses he was carrying down on the table, and held out his hand. "I'm Alec. Is vodka okay for you?"

She shook his hand. "Vodka's great." She peeked at Debbie. "You can keep this one; he's alright in my book."

He went to wrap his arms around her, but Jolie edged back, and her body stiffened.

Alec held his hands up in surrender. "Sorry, I didn't mean—"

Jolie smiled at the familiar face behind him. "Peter. I didn't know you came in here?"

"Is he annoying you?" Peter shook his head at Alec. "You're such an idiot. That's why you never get laid."

Alec bumped Peter's shoulder. "Well, unless it's with your mother."

Peter eyes went wide. "My mum's dead."

"Like I don't own a shovel." Alec grinned.

Jolie and Debbie stared, open-mouthed, as the two men laughed.

"Sorry, ladies. Mum hasn't suddenly died." Peter bent over, and kissed Jolie on the cheek.

She breathed in his heady, woody scent.

"This idiot is my old college roomie. Just ignore him."

"Debbie's already had the pleasure."

His raised his brows, "Really? Okay, then. Do you girls want a drink?"

Jolie looked at her full glass, and before she could speak, Debbie fluttered her eyelashes. "Two vodka and diet cokes, please."

"Be right back." Peter grinned, and dragged his mate away.

Jolie put her hand on her hip, and glared at Debbie. "What are you doing?"

Debbie stepped forward, and hugged Jolie. "You

two would make such a cute couple."

Jolie glared at her. "Don't. Peter's a mate."

"Hmm." Debbie raised an eyebrow.

I'm fond of him... "Stop it. Stop trying to match-make, I don't need to lose one of my best friends by trying to sleep with him. And he's just gone through a bad break-up." She shook her head. "'You and I have been friends forever, how about we settle down, have some kids, make woopee.'"

"Oh, sweetie, I'm not trying to get you married off. I'm only trying to get you laid." Her eyes wandered down to the crotch area of Jolie's jeans. "It's going to heal closed, if you don't use it."

Jolie crossed her hands in front of herself. "Lesbo."

Peter returned with Alec, and the drinks. His smile reached his dark eyes. "You look nice."

Debbie took her drink, and grabbed Alec by the arm. "Come with me a minute?" She hauled him away from the others.

"I'm not sure who should be more afraid, him or her." Peter grinned.

"I think this is their fourth date."

"With our Debbie?"

She nodded. A section of hair fell over her face, and she tucked it behind her ear.

"We're going to decorate Aunt May's kitchen while she is away. I was hoping you would help us? I think Debbie is going to ask..." She noticed the concerned look on his face.

"Sure, I'll help." He took Jolie's hand in his. "What happened?" He stroked the bruises colouring her knuckles and half of her fingers.

"I punched the sink." She shrugged.

Peter tensed. "Why?"

"It wasn't on purpose." She withdrew her hand from his.

Peter sighed. "How did you *accidentally* punch the sink?"

She leaned back, shaking her head. "I found a picture of *him*. I was throwing it in the bin."

Peter laughed. "You always were a bad shot."

Jolie stared down at the floor.

"I'm sorry, I shouldn't have laughed. I know it's hard. You going to be okay?" He wrapped his arms around her, and kissed the top of her head. "He wants his head looking at, messing about on you."

It would have been easy to fall in love with you. She bit her bottom lip. *Am I that desperate and lonely that I'm fixating on my friends?* Jolie needed to get away. Her heart pounded in her ears. She eased out of his embrace. Her confused feelings for her friend caused an internal struggle between her mind and her heart. "I have to go." Her eyes darted about the room. She spotted Debbie in the corner, running her fingers through Alec's hair. "Will you tell Debbie I've gone?"

"Sure, but stay a little while, talk to me?"

She bit down on her bottom lip. "I can't."

"I'll walk you to the taxi rank."

"Don't be daft. It's literally across the road." She leant over, and gave him a quick hug. "I'll see you Monday morning."

Peter's shoulders slumped. "Oh, okay. See you at work.

CHAPTER 5 DECORATING

The car's tires bounced on the old cobbled street. The large redbrick terraced houses still looked like they did when they were built in the 1950s, with big bay windows and small, walled front gardens. Jolie stopped outside number seventy-eight. "You never see kids playing outside anymore." She turned to Debbie. "We were always in the street, playing ball, skipping, or hopscotch."

Debbie smacked her lips together, and smiled at her reflection in the visor mirror. "We didn't have the stuff kids do now."

The large, dark green door opened, and Aunt May stepped out. Sunlight bounced off her jet-black hair, which was cut in a sharp, shoulder-length bob, massive suitcases in each hand. "There're my girls."

Jolie and Debbie got out of the car. "We'll get the cases, Aunt May."

Debbie walked over. "Mum, you look amazing. I love the new haircut and that colour suits you."

"You look hot." Jolie said, and opened the boot of the car. She grunted when she picked a case up. "What the hell do you have in here? It weighs a ton."

Debbie dragged the other case to the car. "You're not kidding. I think she has a body in this one."

"You girls! It's just a few essentials." She fluffed her hair. "Do you think my new haircut might attract some exotic young creature?" Aunt May asked.

"Mum," Debbie shrieked. "Don't you dare! Think

about Dad."

May put her hand on her hip, and pointed at Debbie. "Every night for the last fifteen years, I've thought about yer dad. I have never once been interested in another man, but I am going tae have fun on this holiday. And if I get the attention of any young men, I'm going tae enjoy it." She lowered her hand. "It's not like I'm going to jump into the scratcher with anyone. I just need tae feel like a woman—wanted, desirable."

Jolie gasped as a pain stabbed at her heart. *This is my fault.* She made her way to the front of the car, and got in.

Jolie didn't speak for the rest of the drive to the airport. Nor did she hear a word that was spoken; her mind was fixed on her childhood, and the events which had changed all their lives. When she pulled into the drop-off point, she couldn't remember the journey. They all got out, and went to the back of the car.

"Yer very quiet, honey," Aunt May said.

Jolie turned around to see the worried look on her aunt's face. "I'm okay. I'm just going to miss you."

Aunt May leaned forward, and placed her right hand on Jolie's face. "I'm going to miss you, too." She glanced at Debbie. "Both of you."

Debbie grabbed a trolley, and heaved both cases on it. "Really, Mum, you're only going away for two weeks…aren't you?"

"Yeah, two weeks. Now, give me hug."

As the three of them embraced, a spectacled man in a grey uniform approached.

 He stopped in front of them, with his hands behind his back. "You'll have to move that car," he said, as he peered over his round glasses.

"We're just going," Jolie replied, and let go of May.

The man murmured something incoherent, and walked off, heading towards another family who had just pulled into the drop-off point.

May wrapped her fingers around the trolley's handle. "Give my love to yer dad, and tell him I'll see him next month." She sniffed and wiped the bottom of her nose, her eyes blinking away the moisture.

As Aunt May made her way towards the entrance, Debbie let out a little sob. "Come on. Let's go, before I have to redo my makeup again."

Jolie squeezed her hand. "How's about we go choose the paint for the kitchen."

The girls stood in the paint aisle of the local B & Q DIY store. Debbie was holding up a tin of emerald green emulsion. "But, it's her favourite colour."

"It's too dark. The kitchen is a shoe box, well, it's not a shoe box, but it's small. It will be like the kitchen has a bad cold." Jolie pointed to a pastel mint green colour. "What about that one?"

Debbie put the cans of paint next to each other, and stepped back. She hummed and tapped her finger on her lips.

Jolie huffed, picked up a tin of white gloss for the woodwork, a set of paintbrushes, and a paint roller.

"Okay, the mint one's better," Debbie said.

When they left the store, Jolie stopped dead in her tracks. "What the hell?"

An old man leaned on Jolie's car. Another car was half way up the bonnet of hers. She almost dropped the paint, and had to grip it tight. Panic filled her when the old man wiped his brow. The white handkerchief turned deep red.

Tears threatened to overflow, as she asked him if he was alright. He looked at her, dazed and confused. He kept repeating he didn't know. Sirens wailed in the distance. The blue flashing lights pulled up beside them.

Jolie ran her hand over the driver's door of her little red car. When she turned back, the paramedics had sat the old man down in the ambulance. A man stood taking notes, as the female studied his wound.

Debbie put her hand on her chest. "Holy shit. I'm glad we weren't in that."

Jolie nodded, and walked over to the male paramedic. "Is he okay?"

The man nodded. "Yeah, are you with him?"

"No, it was my car he drove over. He seemed confused."

"We'll check him," he said, and turned away.

A police car drove into the car park, and stopped next to the ambulance. An officer got out, and approached the paramedics. A few minutes later, she saw the paramedic point at her, and the policeman nodded.

He asked her if she was hurt, or had seen what happened.

"No, we just came out, and it was like this."

He thanked her, and gave her an incident number for her insurance.

"What happens now?"

"Call your insurance, and get a tow truck," he said, and walked back to his car.

Debbie appeared at her side. "Peter's coming to pick us up. He said he'll call the garage."

Jolie nodded, but could not take her eyes off the car which appeared to be trying to eat hers.

Peter arrived with Alec, who grabbed hold of Debbie, and placed his forehead against hers. "I was so worried you might have been hurt."

Jolie wiped away a tear, as her emotions got the better of her.

"Hey, you okay?" Peter said.

She chuckled. "Getting soft in my old age. They're perfect for each other."

Peter put the palm of his hand against her head. "Are you sure you weren't in the car?"

Jolie slapped his hand away.

He laughed, and opened the passenger door.

***

Alec was halfway up the wooden ladder, removing bits of wallpaper with a scraper. Peter and Jolie were busy stripping the old fake-tiled wallpaper off the bottom of the walls.

Debbie shovelled the debris into black plastic bags. "Are we going to paint the cupboards first with the gloss paint?"

"What?" Peter asked, "Are you seriously going to paint the cupboards?

Jolie nodded, "Yeah. Nobody likes the old mustard colour."

Alec started laughing, and Debbie slapped the back of his legs.

"It looks awful. Please don't. They have a sale on at Wilkie's Kitchen Wonders. You can get Shaker-style fronts for a tenner each," Peter said.

Debbie pointed at each cupboard, as she counted. "We'd need nine. I can't afford an extra ninety quid. We just paid nearly fifty pounds for the paint, and with Jolie's car…"

"I'll pay. Your mum's been good to me. She

always had a hot meal ready for me, when my mother was having one of her off days." Peter paused.

When your mum was so out of it, she couldn't even answer the door to you? Jolie would never say it aloud. His mother had been clean for the last ten years, but that didn't make the past any better.

Peter shook his head, as if getting rid of a bad memory, and continued, "Let's finish stripping the walls. Alec can fill the holes, and I'll take you both to choose the doors."

It didn't take long for the walls to be stripped, and they made their way to the store.

"I like the white, but I also like the beechwood ones," Debbie said.

Jolie ran her finger over the wooden doors. "The beach one is my favourite."

"That's settled then; we all like the beechwood. Now, are you sure you want Shaker?"

Jolie and Debbie looked at each other and nodded. "Yeah, Mum will love that style."

Peter piled the cupboard fronts onto the trolley.

***

Back at the house, Peter refused to let the girls carry the doors. "You open up, get Alec, and we'll take them inside."

Jolie spun round when she heard Debbie shout, "Alec!"

Jolie and Peter raced into the hallway. Debbie knelt next to Alec, his long dark hair, and clothes covered in green paint. A paint trail of hand and foot prints over the carpet and wall showed his path of destruction.

"What happened?" Jolie asked.

Alec stared at them. "Hi, when did you guys get

back?"

"Are you hurt?" Debbie asked.

"No." His face creased when he lifted his paint-covered hands.

Peter handed his jacket to Jolie and helped Alec stand up. "Come on, mate, let's sit you down on a chair."

Jolie led the way. She gasped as she entered the kitchen. Paint was splashed over the walls, table, and floor. The small portable TV lay on its side, the corner fractured like a spider's web where it had hit the floor, the ladder on top of it.

"At least it's only emulsion," Peter said. He sat Alec down on a chair.

Debbie leant down and kissed his paint covered face.

"I'm okay, but I don't remember falling, or how I got to the hallway."

Debbie ran her hands over his head.

"Ouch!" he cried out, and flinched.

"There's a right lump at the back."

Jolie walked over, and carefully checked out the bump. "We should get you checked out at the hospital."

"No, I'm okay. Really, I am," he insisted.

"I really think you should see a doctor," said Peter.

Alec stood up. "I just want to get cleaned up." He took his shoes and clothes off.

"I'll take him to the shower. Will you take care of this?" Debbie said.

"Of course, pass me his clothes. I'll get them washed. Uncle Mike's stuff should fit him."

Jolie threw the clothes in the washer, as Peter

started scooping what paint he could back into the tin. Then, Jolie filled the mop bucket, while Peter took the T.V. and ladders outside.

She had to change the water in the mop bucket three times, but finally, the table, sides, and floor were paint-free. She heard Peter call from the hall.

His bum wiggled, as he scrubbed away at the carpet.

"What did you say?"

He sat back on his haunches. "The paint is coming out of the carpet, but we will need to decorate the walls, can't wipe it off the 70s woodchip wallpaper."

Jolie giggled. "Don't take the mick, that's a classic."

"Have you got any old towels so I can dry off the carpet?"

She ran upstairs, and grabbed some towels from the airing cupboard next to the bathroom. She paused, as she heard Debbie giggling away. Smiling, she went back down to the hall. They placed the towels on the floor, and stamped over them.

***

"*Of course* you had to get in the shower with him," Jolie said. Debbie and Alec's wet hair dripped, and damp patches appeared on their clothes. Alec laced his fingers through Debbie's.

"The place looks great," Debbie said.

Jolie pointed at a paintbrush. "There's a full wall left. You've been up there nearly two hours."

Debbie wrapped her arm around Alec. "Sorry."

"It was all her. I was injured, and she took advantage of me, terrible girl," Alec said, pulling Debbie towards him, and kissing her.

"Well, you look alright now. You two can finish this room, we," Jolie pointed from herself to Peter, "are going for fish and chips."

"I'm certainly hungry now," Debbie said. Alec started kissing her neck, causing her to giggle like a school girl.

Peter climbed down from the ladder, and put the paint roller in the tray. "Better let Debbie do the ladder work."

***

Jolie and Peter sat in his car, Jolie munching on chips. "We should get back. Their food is going to be cold."

"Serves them right. They shouldn't have left us to do most of the work." He winked at her. "Let's hope they're finished by the time we get there."

Jolie's eyes went wide. "Peter Day, you have an evil streak in you." *And I like it.*

He passed her a can of beer. "I can be a bad boy, when I want."

Jolie laughed. "I wasn't sure about your mate at first, but I really think he's good for Debbie. She doesn't want to see anyone else. She's changed. I reckon it might even be love."

Peter nodded, and took a swig of beer. "All he ever talks about is Debbie. Debbie did this, and Debbie went there. It's weird. He was always a bit of a player."

"So was she. I'm happy for her." *I wish I could be that happy with a guy.*

The engine roared to life. "Me, too," Peter said.

***

Debbie was sat on Alec's knee, she ran her fingers through his hair, as he placed light kisses along her shoulders. Jolie checked the wall. "Wow, you actually took time out and painted."

"Yah, all finished," Alec said.

Peter eyed Alec. "It'll need a second coat, and we have to paint the hallway now, thanks to your handiwork."

They all groaned at his joke.

"It's one-coat paint," Debbie said.

"Yeah, it is, but we still have the hallway." Jolie put the food and beer on the table, and Peter placed a small flat screen T.V. on the floor.

Debbie pointed to the T.V. "Whose is that?"

"It's the one from my bedroom. It never gets used, and Aunt May likes to watch her cookery programs and cook." Jolie staggered backwards, as Debbie jumped up from Alec's lap and flung her arms around her.

"She is going to be so happy. Thank you."

"I'll get the old sheets from the car to cover the carpet, then we can start in the hallway, and let the lovebirds eat."

The last screw turned on the latch. Jolie stood back smiling, admiring the kitchen, Peter, and his work. Alec stood behind Debbie, his arms wrapped around her waist, his chin on her shoulder. A feeling of jealousy quickly passed as Jolie wished for someone to hold her. Her heart skipped a beat when Peter stood up and winked at her. She shook her head. *Seriously, get a grip, you stupid cow.*

***

Later that evening, Jolie sat with her feet tucked under her legs. She placed the mug of hot chocolate on the side table, and switched the laptop on. She blinked at the brightness of the screen when it came to life. She Googled 'love on the internet.'

Dozens and dozens of stories popped up. A photo caught her attention of a smiling family, a young couple with a white-blonde toddler. The headline: *I Found My One in a Million.*

"I met my wife on One in a Million, five years ago. I had been living outside of the city in a rural area. I dated a few of the women in the village, and it wasn't working out; we didn't click. I decided to try online dating. I figured before subscribing to a pay service like the Big Groups, I'd try One in a Million. I had some really, really awful dates at first, I almost gave up. However, one of the respondents was taking over the rural veterinarian practice, so I thought, why not? If she loves animals, that's a start. We dated for a year, got married, and last year, our family was complete when our son arrived."

Jolie moved on to the next story, and photo of a middle-aged couple grinning, their crow's feet mirroring one another. Their headline: *The Long-Term Couple, Who Met After Just One Week of Online Dating!*

"The most amazing part for me was how we found each other so quick. We both decided to try online dating, and, within our first week, we met each other. We still both dated other people in that first week, but I knew I had found the man I wanted to spend the rest of my life with. We have been together ten years."

Jolie "aww'd," as she took a sip of hot chocolate. The next story didn't have a photo but the headline caught her attention: *Printed in the Stars.*

It's great that they all have happy endings, but the stories are so cheesy. Might be worth a shot. Jolie read the next story.

"I put an advert in the paper, 'Professional man,

aged thirty, seeks female twenty-five to thirty-five for long-term relationship. Must be non-smoker and like dogs.' That was all I put, and the number of people who responded was amazing. I thought I would get a few weirdos, but I think there was only one. I went on a few dates, but they weren't really my type. Then, I went out with the woman, who had signed her name, 'P.' It was love at first sight, and as the night went on, she completely stole my heart. I wouldn't change a thing about her, she's perfect. I tell her everyday how lucky I am to have her in my life, and how much I love her. We have twin girls, who will be two next month. I have never been happier."

She ran her finger over the words on the screen. "I want someone to feel like that about me. You win, Debbie. I'm going to try online dating." Her hand trembled, as she took another drink from her cup.

CHAPTER 6 UNCLE MIKE

Hiding under the small, round dining table, she hugged herself, and tried to make her body as tiny as possible. Her lip stung as it rubbed against her knees. She could taste the mix of metallic blood and salty tears.

"Mama!" she cried out, when her mother fell to the floor. She took a sharp breath, and squeezed her knees.

"This is your fault, little bitch." He lifted the glass, the brown liquid sloshing about, then his arm swung backwards.

She cringed at the movement, and closed her eyes. Her face stung as pieces of glass hit her cheek. Her body trembled, urine dripped down her leg onto the floor. She could smell his stale breath, but she refused to open her eyes.

The door shuddered. "Jolie!" The loud bangs and shouting continued.

Her eyes sprung open.

The front door flew wide, light poured into the room.

She was safe. "Uncle Mike!"

Jolie woke with a start. She sat up, and looked around the room, trying to find comfort in her surroundings. Tears flooded down her face. The dream was still so vivid in her mind; she could almost smell the whisky. *He can't hurt you ever again.*

Text me before you leave—Deb.

Jolie glanced at the clock. "Shit, seven-forty-five." She kicked the covers off, and replied,

I'll be leaving in twenty minutes.

***

Jolie sat reading in the car outside Debbie's ground

floor apartment. Peter had lent her his car for the day. She flipped the pages of her book. She became so engrossed in the story she held her breath, as she read about the ghostly figure creeping out of the wall. She was so emerged in the pages that when Debbie tapped on the window, she screamed, and her hand flew to her chest.

Giggling, Debbie opened the door, and got in. She placed her pink leather handbag on her lap. "Why do you read those ghost stories?"

Jolie smirked. "It wasn't the story that scared me, it's you—you look like crap."

"You don't look so hot yourself. Did you sleep?"

Jolie shook her head. "Not much."

Debbie rubbed her arm. "Nightmares, again?"

Jolie shuddered.

"Want to talk about it?"

"I'd rather not. Where's Alec?"

"Still sleeping." She flipped the passenger sun visor down, adjusted it, and looked in the small mirror. "I *do* look like crap." She unzipped her bag, and pulled out her foundation. "Nothing I can't handle."

Jolie put her book in the back seat of the car, then started the engine. "We only have a couple of hours." She suppressed a grin. "Are you sure it'll be enough time to fix all of your face?"

Debbie slapped her on the thigh.

Jolie giggled. "Hey! Don't distract the driver, your face is doing that already. Hurry up with the make-up,"

Debbie stuck out her tongue, and picked up the tube of foundation.

The two girls stood outside the imposing building. Red brick walls, with cream-rounded tops, stood forty feet high. A prominent ventilation tower soared up to the sky from behind the walls.

The enormous metal doorway gave Jolie the shivers. No matter how many times she had been to visit Strangeways Prison, she always got the jitters before going in. She turned to Debbie. "You do have your passport this time?"

Debbie huffed. "One time, three years ago—of course I have it!"

They waited for the doors to open, and walked inside.

After she had been frisked by the guards, Jolie took a deep breath, and made her way through the double doors leading to the visitor area.

The familiar sting of guilt stabbed at Jolie's heart. She glanced from the Formica tables, to the pale walls, then to prison guards in their blue uniforms. People sat talking with the prisoners, who were wearing orange inmate vests. The large room had enough space and tables to hold 40 visitors and inmates.

She smiled, as a man in his fifties, with greying hair and gold framed glasses, waved at her. She sat down opposite him. "Uncle Mike."

"Jolie, you look prettier every time I see you." He grabbed her hand, and gave it a gentle squeeze. "Where's Debbie?"

She rolled her eyes. "Trying to persuade the guard to let her bring in an extra box of chocolates."

Mike laughed. "Every single visit." His eyes lit up, as he peered over Jolie's shoulder. "Debbie."

"Hi, Dad, couldn't get the gay one to change his

mind about the rum truffles."

Mike glared at Debbie over his glasses. "You were trying to bring in liquors?"

Debbie waved her hand in the air. "Trying, yeah, but they're so stuffy, these guards."

Jolie bumped Debbie's shoulder. "Unbelievable."

Mikes shook his head. "You girls make my day. What news of the world beyond the wall?"

"Aunt May is on a cruise, and while she was away, we decorated the kitchen as a surprise."

"She told me about the cruise on her last visit. Hey, you girls are wonderful. That's lovely thing to do for her, she'll be so happy." He swallowed loudly.

Debbie crossed her arms. "I'm not happy about the cruise."

Mike scowled at her. "Why on Earth not? You two have been away a few times."

Jolie decided to change the subject. "Any news on the parole hearing?"

"They've given me the fifteenth of December."

Debbie clapped her hands together. "You'll be home for Christmas."

"Let's not be hasty now." He patted Debbie's hand.

Someone shouted, "It's you."

Jolie looked over her shoulder. Bernie, the guy who had been screaming about demons outside the pub, stood staring at her, that same toothless grin on his face as the last time she saw him. He pointed his bony index finger at her. "It's you. I'm—"

Mike bolted up out of his seat. "Leave the girl alone, Bernie," he growled.

A prison officer eyed Mike, and placed his hand on Bernie's shoulder. "Calm down."

"I have to talk to her. She needs to know," Bernie begged.

Jolie jumped when Mike put his hand on her arm. "Ignore him, love, he's not all there."

She watched in horror, as Bernie started screaming. "Have to stay away, have to stay!" He tried pulling out of the officer's grip, his eyes never leaving hers. Another officer ran over, and dragged him to the floor.

"You girls get out of here," Mike said.

Jolie couldn't look away from the old man's intense eyes. Debbie put her arm around Jolie, who gasped at the contact.

She gave her a gentle squeeze. "Come on, let's go."

As the girls approached the car, Jolie asked, "What the hell was all that about?"

"Maybe they thought a riot might start?"

Jolie shook her head. "I'm not stupid. I meant the way Bernie acted. And what was he doing in there?"

Debbie shrugged her shoulders. "I have no idea, maybe he was arrested for being drunk again? I remember Molly going visiting him in prison once before. He had got so drunk, he smashed nearly all the windows in three shops. I don't think he's dangerous, though, so don't worry."

Jolie bit her thumbnail. "What's Molly got to do with it?"

"You know he's some relation to Molly? He used to pick her up from school, now and then."

Jolie's stomach turned over. "My god. I didn't recognize him. It must be about ten…maybe twelve years since I last saw him. She would never talk about him when I asked her who he was."

"Maybe he's her grandad? She was always embarrassed by him, falling over, and wearing stinking, dirty clothes. Shame."

CHAPTER 7 INTERNET DATING

"You have a hit," Debbie squealed from the study.

Jolie gingerly edged her way over to Debbie, and peered over her shoulder at the PC.

"Carl Nanos, athletic, enjoys going to the movies, loves Italian and Greek food, and likes to travel. And look at his profile picture. Meow, he's a Greek Adonis. Looks like a young Alcide."

Jolie wiped her forehead. "Who?"

"Alcide, that werewolf guy," Debbie purred.

Jolie took a step back, and glanced at her shaking hands. *Oh god, calm down.* "I can't do this."

"Hey, don't back out now! Just talk to him. At least send him a message."

Jolie started biting her thumbnail. "What would I say?"

"You're hopeless." Debbie laughed. "Leave it to me." She started typing away.

The clicking of the keyboard sent shivers down Jolie's spine. "But, I have that blind date next week with your boss's brother."

"Now, you have a date on Saturday," Debbie wafted her hand towards the screen, "with Carl "the Greek Adonis" Nanos."

Jolie looked up at the ceiling, as bile rose in her throat. "I can't do this."

Debbie stood, and took hold of Jolie's right hand. "You're only twenty-four. Live a little. It'll be an adventure!"

"I was with Dave for seven years. This isn't exciting; it's downright scary." She pulled her hand out of Debbie's, and sat down on the couch, hugging herself. "I've never been with another man."

Debbie sat down next to her, leaned over, and stroked her hair. "It's like riding a bike. Especially if you get on top and control the speed."

***

Saturday afternoon came far too quickly for Jolie. She sat obediently, allowing Debbie to give her the makeover she'd insisted on. "I don't need all this, just make sure there's plenty of concealer." She wriggled about in the chair, and tried to pull the mini skirt down over her thighs. "This is far too short. I've got belts that are bigger. And who plans a date on a Saturday afternoon?"

"Stop moaning. That skirt is so cute on you; the white shows off your tanned skin. And the Jimmy Choos show off your legs."

"I do love these shoes. The diamantes remind me of sparkling rain on a dark, dismal day."

Debbie pulled a stray hair from Jolie's black, camisole top. "I wish you would wear something tighter, show off those bad boys. Pity none of my tops will fit you."

"The…skirt is bad enough, thank you." Jolie felt the colour drain from her face when the doorbell chimed. She took a deep breath, and slowly released it. "That's my taxi. I'll text you his car number plate. If you don't hear from me every hour, phone the police," she said, and walked out.

Jolie sat in the back of the taxi, legs crossed with her knees bobbing up and down. *What if he's a psycho? Or worse, into strange rituals and kinky crap?* She fanned her hand in front of her face. *I can't breathe. It's so hot in here.*

"That'll be four pounds exactly, love."

Jolie glanced up blinking; she hadn't noticed the taxi had stopped. She handed him a five-pound note, and told him to keep the change.

She stood in front of the coffee shop, her hands trembling, as she clasped her handbag. "Come on, girl. You can do this." She took a deep breath, and opened the door.

A man in his late forties stood smiling, holding a small bunch of pink carnations. His thinning hair, brown corduroy trousers, and black sweatshirt had seen better days.

No, don't you dare be my date!

"Jolie? You look just like your picture," he said.

She stood there open-mouthed, and twisted her head side-to-side, as she desperately tried to find the cute werewolf guy.

"I'm Carl." He held the posies out.

"Hi, erm, thanks." Jolie took the flowers. "You don't look much like your picture."

Carl laughed. "My son…he put his picture up as a joke. Most people don't look like their photo." He smiled, revealing yellow-stained teeth. "Not sure your clothing is right for the date, but shall we go?"

She peered down at her legs and sparkly shoes. "Where are we going?"

"It's a surprise, but you'll like it. I asked the ladies at church, they thought it was a good idea." He nodded his head, then turned towards the door.

As they exited the coffee shop, Carl pointed to an old Land-Rover. "That's the beast." He grinned. "Never lets me down; I've never missed a church service since I got her."

Jolie got her phone out of her bag, and texted the number plate details to Debbie. She opened the car door, held on to the bottom of her skirt, and tried to step in gracefully.

"Your legs are a bit chunky."

Jolie raised her eyebrow. "What?"

"You shouldn't wear such short skirts, if you don't want people to comment."

Jolie folded her arms across her chest. "Women who carry a little extra weight live longer than the men who mention it."

Carl lifted his hands up in surrender. "Whoa there. I never said you were fat. Where did you get that idea from? That wouldn't make me a good Christian, now would it?"

Her face went deadpan. "No, it wouldn't. And who mentioned fat?"

He put his hands on the steering wheel, and winked at her. "Girls are far too skinny these days. What is a size zero anyway?"

Get out of the car, and leave. Her hand went to the door handle; she cringed as the engine rumbled to life. *Damn it.*

They had been driving about twenty minutes, when Carl asked, "Are you a religious person, Jolie?"

"Hmm, what?"

"Do you go to church and pray?"

Jolie laughed. "Me? God, no."

Carl looked her square in the eye. "You should never take the Lord's name in vain." He turned his head back towards the road.

Great, that's all I need, a religious nut. "Your bio didn't mention you were religious?"

"My son thought it best to leave it out, until people get to know me. But, I shouldn't have listened to him. He blasphemes all the time, my wife used to as well…before she died."

Jolie thought she heard him whimper. "I'm sorry. You must miss her."

"I miss her every day. Cancer is not something you want to watch your loved ones go through." A gentle smile crossed his face. "She's been gone five years now."

Poor guy. Maybe I'm being a little harsh?

He grinned. "We're almost there."

The Land-Rover stopped at an off-road car park, at The Edale Skyline in the Peak district. Carl switched the engine off, and looked at Jolie. "There's a bric-a-brac sale on after service at my church tomorrow. It's usually fun. You could come to the service, and then, after, meet the gang." His head bobbed up and down, like a nodding dog in a car window.

"Church isn't my thing; I thought you got that earlier." She saw the sad expression in his eyes. "But, thanks for the offer," she added, as she opened the car door.

"It's never too late to rekindle your faith."

Jolie scanned the wide-open space and lush green hills, as she slid out of the car. She balled her hands into fists, to try and stop them shaking. *Oh god, if he did something to me here, no one would hear me scream.* "Why are we here?"

"Your profile said you like hiking." He opened his arms out wide. "This is perfect."

Jolie looked down at her feet. Her heels had started slowly sinking into the soft grass. "I'm in a miniskirt and three-inch high heels."

Carl's face dropped, and the colour left his cheeks. "I messed up. I'm such an idiot."

Oh, for goodness sake. "No, really, it was a great idea, I just wished you had said what you had planned."

"I'd also planned to go to the cinema afterwards. You like films, right?" Tears brimmed in his eyes.

Jolie tensed. "Is there an earlier showing for the film?" *Shit, I can't believe I just asked that.*

Carl smiled, and rubbed his hands together. "Yes, yes, there is."

Oh, goodie.

Carl skipped around the car, and got in the driver's side.

Jolie opened the door on her side. Her shoe stuck in the mud, and her leg wobbled. She grabbed for the door, but only grasped at thin air and tumbled backwards. She landed with a thud, and a slight pain shot up her back. "Ouch. Damn it."

Carl leant out of the open passenger door. "What are you doing down there?"

"I'm catching some rays. Maybe I'll even grab a glass of wine while I'm down here." She stood up, craning her neck trying to look at the back of her skirt. She spun it round, and groaned at the large, damp, football-sized grass and mud stain.

As they drove back towards town, Carl spoke of his love for the lord and his church. Jolie stayed quiet, and tried her best to tune him out with thoughts about how she wished he was a werewolf. And what the actor who played Alcide was really like.

***

Carl and Jolie walked into the cinema foyer. He

stopped, looked her up and down, and said, "I only really date Christian women. You are my first non-believer." Then, he walked over to the middle-aged woman behind the counter. "One please." He handed over a ten-pound note. "Do you serve the sweets and drinks here as well?"

Jolie's head flopped forward. *What a keeper.* He ordered a large popcorn and cola. She got her phone out of her bag, and texted Debbie.

Shut my profile down, now!

He playfully lent on the counter, laughing, and picked up a crucifix next to the register. The woman blushed, when she noticed Jolie watching them.

He glanced over his shoulder at her briefly, then turned back towards the woman. "Oops, 'the date,' I'd almost forgotten about her." He bent closer to the woman, and lowered his voice. "She's not one of us. And not that much fun."

Jolie ground her teeth together. *Cheeky bugger. It was all, oh, feel sorry for me, then someone else grabs your attention. I'm the idiot.*

He picked up his popcorn and drink, turned towards Jolie. "You better hurry up and get your stuff, if you don't want to miss the start of the film."

Jolie lifted her arms up in the air. "I'm done. You can't treat people like this. I didn't want to hurt your feelings, you being a Christian. But, going to church doesn't make you a Christian, any more than standing in a garage makes you a friggin' car."

He called her name, as she stormed off. It took all the power she could muster to stop herself from slapping the gormless look off his face.

Outside, she flagged a taxi down. She huffed and sighed, annoyed with herself for being so weak, allowing this stranger to manipulate her. And the fact she had actually walked into the cinema wearing a dirty skirt.

When she got home, she slammed her apartment door shut, grabbed a bottle of wine from the kitchen, and slipped into her PJs.

The next day, she called Debbie, and demanded she shut down the profile, getting more and more annoyed at Debbie's giggles, as she relayed the story. She couldn't face the outside world today. She took her duvet into the living room, opened a tin of chocolates and a bottle of cola, and stuck a DVD in the player.

***

Jolie woke early Monday morning, she grabbed her running gear, and got dressed.

The trees rustled, and the cool wind bit at her face, as she raced around the park. Her heart rate soared when she saw the blond man in the distance watching her. *Dave?* She stopped, and squinted in the man's direction. A dog barked behind her. She jumped when a couple of runners ran past. She closed her eyes, and took a deep breath. When she opened them, the man who had been watching her was gone. She decided to go home and have a shower, before her imagination got out of control.

When Jolie arrived at work, a grin spread across her face, as she sniffed the air, and was greeted by an aromatic sweet coffee blend emanating from the kitchenette at the back of the reception.

She eyed the mail stacked up ready for her to open, and trailed her fingers over the uneven texture of the red brick wall.

Peter appeared in the doorway, holding two mugs

of coffee. "You really are very strange. Fish and brick fetish. But, never mind the weird stuff. How was the date?"

Her handbag made a thud, when she dropped it beside the stack of mail. "Don't ask. A disaster."

Peter laughed, as he walked over to her. "You're still alive, aren't you?" He held a cup out to her.

"A bit of my soul died. And that's not the worst part." Jolie cupped the warm coffee between her hands, closed her eyes, and breathed in the sweet chocolate from the mocha latte. "Hmmm, this is just heaven. And you even put it in a real cup."

Peter sat down on the burgundy leather couch in the spacious reception area. The cup clinked on the glass table. He patted the seat next to him. "Come on, tell Uncle Peter all about."

Jolie screwed her nose up at him. "So you can take the mickey out of me all day..." Jolie's phone rang. "It's Debbie." She pushed the *accept call* button. "Morning, Debbie."

"Why did you tell Molly you're not going to the party?"

Jolie blushed, and looked over at Peter. "It's not my kind of thing."

"Nothing normal is your kind of thing. It's not sleazy, just some play things and lingerie."

She gave a loud sigh. "I'm not going to get out of this, am I?"

"Nope, I'll tell Molly we'll be there."

The phone went dead, and her heart hammered in her chest. *This is almost as bad as online dating. All those lady toys. Oh crap.*

The leather creaked, as Peter leant forward. "Well, what's our Darling Debbie got in store for you next?"

Jolie slumped down on the couch. "A Lady Lace party."

Peter shook his head. "Don't mention that name to me. Worst experience of my life."

Jolie sat up straight and smiled. "I'm all ears."

His face went bright red, and he loosened his grey silk tie. "You'd better not spread this around?"

Jolie crossed her heart. "Promise."

"Last year." He took in a deep breath. "Cassie decided we needed to spice up our love life."

She rolled her eyes at hearing Cassie's name.

"She insisted I go with her to the Lady Lace and rubber shop. I was the only bloke in there."

Jolie took a sip of her drink.

Peter ran his fingers through his hair, and licked his lips. "She kept picking things up, and calling the shop assistant over for advice. I kept my head down the whole time, just peeking up whenever she mentioned my name."

Jolie patted his leg. "Poor baby." She pulled her hand away, before she gave his leg a squeeze. *Get a grip, concentrate on the story.* She swallowed the pooling saliva in her mouth, when she stared into his eyes. *You really are gorgeous. If we weren't such good friends…Oh, for god sakes, get a grip.* She bit her bottom lip, and wriggled in her seat.

Peter was saying something about a guy in a wig and red high heels. She shook her head, and tried to concentrate on the story.

"He told the woman at the counter he wanted his money back on the anal balls, as they don't work."

"Oh my god. Did I hear right? A guy in drag returned anal balls?" She watched him nervously scratch the stubble on his chiselled chin. *You always do that when you are embarrassed. It's quite cute.*

"Yeah, I couldn't stop staring at him. I started to walk away, when I caught my foot on the dildo display unit."

She burst out laughing, and quickly covered her mouth with her hand.

Peter glared at her.

"Sorry." She sniggered.

"What could I do? I couldn't just leave them for the shop assistant to put away. There were dozens and dozens of them, everywhere. So, as I'm helping her balance numerous rubber dicks, of all shapes and sizes, back on the shelf, in walks my mother."

"Your mum? I *so* wish I had been there."

Peter pursed his lips at her, and nudged her with his shoulder. "It's not funny. I had hold of this pink rubber thing, I swear, it was two-foot-long and wobbled about like it was made of jelly. It kept bouncing around, like it had a life of its own."

She bent over, holding her stomach, tears streaming down her face.

Peter turned his head away, and crossed his arms over his chest. "You're as bad as my mother. I thought she was going to wet herself, she laughed that much."

Jolie sat up straight, and wiped her eyes. "What was your mum doing there in the first place?"

"I have no idea, and I wasn't going to ask her." Peter stood up. "I have work to do."

"I'm sorry, but it was funny." *This is what I need. A friend, nothing complicated.*

"It's good to hear you laugh again, even if it is at me."

Jolie stood up, reached up on her tiptoes, and gave

him a quick peck on the cheek. She paused at the familiar smell of his woody aftershave. His body stiffened. She jerked her head away.

The outside office door slammed shut. Jolie glimpsed a man walking past the floor to ceiling window. "Was that Dave?"

Peter's jaw tensed. "Yeah."

Jolie cast her eyes downward. *What the hell was he doing here?*

Peter placed his hand in the small of her back. "Are you okay?" She nodded, but he narrowed his eyes. "You don't have to be afraid of him anymore."

"I'm not afraid of him." The phone rang at reception.

"I'll get it," Peter said.

"No, I'm okay. It's my job." She gave him a weak smile.

The day dragged, her heart skipping a beat every time the door opened. On a couple of occasions, she thought she spotted Dave watching her from across the street, but by the time she had come from behind the reception desk, there was no one about. By the end of the day, she was even looking forward to the Lady Lace party, to take her mind off things.

The smell of sickly sweet perfume and alcohol-infused fruit cocktails were thick in the air, when the girls arrived at Molly's house.

Molly swayed about, with a bright pink bra over her black t-shirt, and a pair of matching pink lacy knickers on her head, covering her spiky purple hair. She waved at the two women, as they entered.

"Welcome ladies," she slurred. She stumbled, and landed on her knees. She held her hand up, and shouted, "I'm okay."

Jolie grabbed Molly's arm, and helped her stand up.

"Hey, Molly, let's sit down," she said, and edged her towards the couch.

Debbie winked at Jolie. "I'll get us some drinks."

"Just orange juice for me," Jolie replied, and sat Molly down.

Molly held her empty glass up. "I'll have a sex on the beach."

Jolie looked around the room. A tall, slim woman, whose legs seemed go on forever, was modelling a black thong, bra, suspenders, and lace-topped stockings. She stood with her hands on her hips. Jolie couldn't take her eyes off the woman's perfect, apple-sized breasts, and delicate cleavage.

The woman smiled at her.

Jolie blushed. *Shit. Oh god, how embarrassing. Not only does she have the perfect body....Shit, I'm turning lesbian now.*

"That outfit is available in black, white, and pink. And, no, the stockings don't come in pink I'm afraid, ladies," the middle-aged hostess said, and thanked the young model.

Jolie looked up, and watched the slim girl walking away. Her perky butt didn't even wobble. How she envied her.

Her mouth fell open when she saw the table on the other side of the living room was full of rubber-shaped penises in different colours. They ranged from a few inches tall to what she guessed must have been at least a foot long.

"Okay, ladies, whilst our model is changing, shall we have some fun?" the hostess called out.

Jolie sat down next to Molly, her head buzzing

with the noise around her, as women laughed and shouted over each other.

Jolie craned her neck towards the hostess, when someone shouted, "Oh, my god, did you see the size of that mother? That would tear me in half." Laughter erupted in the room. She bobbed up and down, and moved from side-to-side, but she couldn't see the offending item.

Debbie came back with the drinks, and laughed. "I think I may have found my new best friend. Black, ribbed, and guaranteed to please."

Molly elbowed Jolie in the side. Molly's left leg banged down on the floor, and she laughed, sliding down the couch. "I'm going to get a closer look," she slurred.

Debbie put the drinks down on the smoked-glass coffee table, and held her hand out to Jolie. "Come on."

Jolie blushed.

"Prude."

"Hussy," Jolie replied, and took hold of her hand.

The two of them walked over to the hostess. Someone handed Molly a cup of black coffee.

Molly took the lacy panties off her head, and flopped down to the floor. Coffee spilled, as she wiped her brow.

Debbie handed Jolie a black Basque, with delicate red bows down the sides, and a matching thong. "This would look so hot on you."

Jolie took hold of it, and held it up to the hostess. "What do you have that will make my thighs look thinner, and flatten my stomach? Maybe a little bit plainer than this?"

The hostess shook her head. "What are you...I'm

guessing a size twelve?"

Jolie nodded.

"That's an American size eight." She smiled. "Does that sound big?"

Jolie felt her face start to burn up. "It's been commented I have…chunky thighs."

Debbie tutted. She squeezed the top of Jolie's right leg. "They're solid, athletic — not chunky."

The hostess lifted her long baggy top up, to reveal a pair of leggings stretched to the limit. The material near the seam was almost transparent. "You don't have chunky thighs." She slapped the top of her leg, and the flesh bounced back and forth. "That's chunky thighs." She laughed. "And they look great draped over my husband's shoulders."

Molly approached them, with red plastic lips covering hers. "Look, watch." The lips started vibrating.

"What are they for?" Jolie laughed.

Debbie rolled her eyes, and the hostess grinned. "Think about it, what would you put in your gob?"

Jolie's eyes went wide. "Seriously?"

Molly took the vibrating lips off. "I'm getting these for Monty."

"Who's Monty?" Debbie, Jolie, and the hostess asked in unison.

"My new fella. His family is minted."

Debbie put her hands on her hips, and rolled her shoulders back. "When did you get a new fella? And how the hell have you sobered up so quickly?"

Jolie giggled. "She's always been the same. Give her another drink, and she'll be falling over again like a lunatic. It's sickening." She picked up a set of lips.

"And that's how I roll," Molly humorously

retorted, and held her middle finger up. She wiggled her hips, and walked away.

Jolie found the on switch, and slipped the soft plastic over her own lips.

Loud banging on the front door drowned out the laughter and merriment from the group. Jolie watched Molly answer the door.

Molly shouted, "Dad!"

Bernie staggered in, blood pouring from a cut on his swollen nose and mouth.

The room went silent, even the dildos seemed to wilt in people's hands.

His half-crazed eyes searched the room, stopping when they found Jolie.

The lips fell away from Jolie's mouth, and landed in her crotch. She grabbed them, and hid them at her side. She clenched her hand, and heard a crack.

Molly placed her hand on his arm; he cowered and covered his face. "What happened, Dad?"

Tears built up in his eyes, as he hurriedly departed the house.

Molly ran after him, calling his name. She walked back inside, grabbed a bottle of wine, and drank from it. "Come on, people, it's a party. Have fun! Don't worry about an old drunk."

Jolie sat Molly down. "Are you okay?"

"Why wouldn't I be?" She took another swig from the bottle.

"You called him, 'Dad'?"

"Frank's my dad. Bernie's, well, he's just a drunk—the sperm donor, my mum calls him." A tear trickled down her cheek. "My mum split up with him before I was born. He had an affair. Frank's my stepdad, but he has been there for me since I was a baby."

"Do you want to go and find him? He looked hurt?"

"No. He probably just fell over."

The host cried out, "Who spilled coffee on my white crotchless knickers?"

Molly put her hand over her mouth. "That was me, shit."

Jolie pulled the plastic lips from her pocket. "You've ruined her crotch, and I've broken her lips."

They both burst out laughing.

"What are you two carrying on about?" Debbie asked.

Jolie linked her arm through Debbie's. "The dangers of being too sexy. Now do you see the plus side to my batman knickers?"

CHAPTER 8 MEMORIES

Jolie locked her apartment door, and joined Debbie out on the street.

A cool summer breeze lifted Jolie's hair across her face. She curved the loose strands behind her ear. "Aren't you cold?" she asked.

"It's like seventy degrees out here." Debbie put her hand on Jolie's forehead. "Are you coming down with something?"

"I don't think so. I'm okay, just a little cold," Jolie replied, and lifted the sleeve of her thin, camel-coloured jacket and checked her watch. "What is keeping Peter? It's nearly three."

"Stop panicking, he'll be here. Not everyone has to be an hour early for everything. Mum's flight doesn't land till four. It's only a twenty-minute drive."

"I hate being late. And Peter drives like an old lady. Honestly, I could fart, and get there quicker under my own steam." She paced back and forth. "I'll be glad to get my car back from the garage later." She popped her hands in the front pockets of her baggy, boyfriend-style jeans. "Was that date number six last night with Alec?"

Debbie's eyes lit up. "Yeah, he's good. Well, you know the old saying? Having sex is like playing bridge. If you don't have a good partner, you'd better have a good hand." Debbie grabbed hold of Jolie's hands, turned them palms up, and chuckled. "As I suspected, callouses…"

Ignoring her, Jolie pulled her hands away, and looked down the street. The red brick walls of the houses were in stark contrast to the black tar road. She spotted the black four-by-four turn the corner. "Here he is."

Debbie jumped up and down, clapping her hands together. "Yay, panic over."

"Whatever." Jolie stood back, as the car drew up to the curb. "Are you planning on another date with Alec?"

Debbie nodded, and they got into the back seats of Peter's car. The familiar smell of leather caused her to subconsciously run her hand over the seats. Then, a strange smell caught her attention. "Have you changed your aftershave?"

She watched Peter's cheeks turn pink. "I'm not wearing aftershave; it's a new deodorant."

Jolie glanced at the rear-view mirror. His dark eyes locked on to hers. "It's nice."

He cleared his throat, and put the car in gear, setting off.

Debbie elbowed her, and grinned. "Put your seatbelt on. This could get wild."

Jolie looked to the right to grab the seat belt, and saw a figure in the window of the house opposite her apartment. She sucked in a breath. *Dave?* She turned towards Debbie, who was texting away on her phone, and then back to the window, but the curtains were closed. Shaking her head, she locked the seatbelt in place. *I'm going crazy. I'm seeing him everywhere. Maybe it wasn't him, just someone wearing the same Medusa face t-shirt I got him for Valentine's.* She smiled, as the memory played out in her mind.

She had just left her office, and walked down the street to the bakery at the corner to grab some lunch. She always found the walk depressing when she was missing Dave. The grey sky loomed above. The empty cars on both sides of the road made her feel closed in.

She smiled when her 'shine bright like a diamond,' ring tone went off.

"Hi, Dave, great timing. I just switched my phone online for Facetime. I miss you." She blew a kiss at the screen.

"I miss you, too. But, you get to see my hunky face now." He winked at the screen.

She ran her fingers through her hair.

"You look gorgeous. Stop panicking, because I can see you."

"Sorry." She gave a nervous chuckle. "Did my present arrive?"

"Yeah. I haven't opened it yet. You'll have to work for mine." He raised an eyebrow.

Jolie pouted. "What? That's not fair. Why can't you come home, and give it to me?"

Dave laughed so loud, she winced. "Believe me, I would love to give it to you right now."

Jolie's mouth fell open. She quickly scanned the area around her, then turned back to the screen. "Hey, I'm in a public place."

"Yeah, sorry. I've set up an email account for you. I'll text you the clues. I've got to go. Love you."

She fought to stop her eyes from watering. "I love you, too. Can't you come home?" The call ended. She sniffed, and wiped her nose with the back of her hand.

Jolie got a cheese sandwich and a bottle of water from the bakery, and headed back to work. The day seemed brighter, and even the street full of parked cars friendlier.

She sat at the table at her work's little kitchenette. Her phone vibrated. A text came through from Dave.

'Email is Jolielovesdave@priceless.com. The password is seven letters, all capitals. Clue number one: What do the song, Leave Right Now, a film with Robin Williams and Matt Damon in it, and the actor who played Jay in Men in Black, have in common?'

She took a bite of her sandwich. "Hmm, Will Smith plays Jay. Will Young sings that song." She Googled the film with Matt Damon and Robin Williams. "Good Will Hunting!" she shouted out loud.

She texted Dave back. 'Easy peasy, it's 'Will.' Next! Only 3 letters to go.'

She sat with her phone in her hand, wiping away the crumbs from her sandwich. No reply. She kept checking the time on the phone. Twenty minutes passed. She sent another text.

'My lunch is over. You are killing me! Next QUESTION, please.'

She stood up, staring at the phone, willing it to vibrate. She sighed, put the phone on the table, then walked over to the coffee pot and poured herself a drink.

Her phone vibrated. Coffee spilt on to the counter top when she slammed the cup down in her rush to get to her phone.

'I am a vowel, you will find me in the name of a film with Owen Wilson, Kate Hudson, and Matt Dillon.'

She chewed on the inside of her bottom lip and rubbed her chin. Picking up a cloth, she wiped up the spillage, then grabbed her mug, and walked back out to reception, whilst typing one handed into her search engine.

"You, Me, and Dupree." Her eyes narrowed and her forehead became creased. "You, me and...it's a vowel, You." She put her hand over her mouth. "Will you."

She sat down at her desk, and switched the PC on. Her hands shook so much she could hardly type in the email address and password.

The first email she saw was from Dave. 'Move in with me.' Disappointment swept over her.

Peter walked past reception. "Hey, I'm going out for a couple of hours to meet a client." He walked closer to the desk. "Are you okay?"

Jolie gave a forced smile. "Yeah, I thought Dave was going to propose, but he just asked me to move in with him."

Peter's jaw tensed. "You don't want to rush into anything."

"Five years is hardly rushing things."

Peter shrugged, and turned away. "I'll be back at three."

She quickly typed a reply back to Dave. *'You arse, you know what I thought you were going to ask!'*

The hours dragged on, without a reply from Dave. Eventually, she left the office for the day, and walked over to her car. There was a single red rose on the windshield. Jolie picked it up, held it to her nose, and sniffed at the gentle fragrance. She glanced up and down the street, but didn't see anyone the rose could've been from.

When she got in the car, she placed the rose on the passenger seat, and sent a text to Dave.

'Did you get someone to leave a rose on my windscreen?'

Dave hadn't replied by the time she arrived at her apartment. A strong flowery scent met her when she opened her front door. She gasped at the sight. From the doorway, right through her hall, the wooden floor was covered in red rose petals. She followed them, the trail led to the kitchen. Her hands shook when she lifted them to push the kitchen door open. There was Dave, sitting at the kitchen table, a soft amber light from flickering candles making his smile so much sweeter.

Her heart pounded in her chest. "What are doing here? Why didn't you tell me?"

He stood up, and ran his hand over the soft material of his t-shirt. "Thank you for the Versace top, but you shouldn't have spent so much on me when we have a wedding to plan for."

The smile left her face, replaced with confusion. "What?"
He walked over to her, and got down on one knee.

Suddenly, Jolie registered her name being called, and it yanked her out of her memory.

"Jolie?"

Jolie shook her head, and glanced at Peter. "Hmm, what?"

"We're here," Peter said. "Debbie's already gone. You go in. I'll park in the short stay carpark." His brow creased, as he turned, and leaned his arm on the seat. "Are you okay?"

"Sorry, I was miles away." She put her head down, and fumbled with her seat belt.

"Somewhere nice, I hope."

The heat built in her face, as the seat belt popped open. She grabbed the handle. "I will be." She opened the car door, swung her legs out, and ran towards the entrance.

Panic set in, as she watched a man shouting at a cowering woman. An image flashed in her mind of her mother lying on the floor. She breathed in through her nose, the smell of stale sweat, cheap perfume, and cigarettes causing her to hold her breath. She could hear her heart pumping. *She could see her stepfather's contorted face, hear his slurred words.* A man ran past, and banged into her. Her body jerked forward, her hand went to her mouth, and she let out a squeal.

She spied a large white column, and made her way towards it. Leaning against it, trying to calm herself down, she spotted Debbie peering up at the arrivals board. She staggered over to her, her head light, as her stomach turned over. She unzipped her jacket, as the heat threatened to send her dizzy, and took a few deep breaths. "What's…the flight number?"

"She landed thirty minutes ago." Debbie turned around. "What's got you so out of puff?"

"She's already landed? Shit, this is why I like to be early. I'm not out of breath. I was catching up with you, running off like that."

"I did no such thing." Debbie crossed her arms over her chest. "I told you we were here, but you were too busy staring at"—she unfolded her arms, and made quote signs with her fingers—"your mate."

Jolie glared at her. "He's not my mate. And you know I don't like to be in these places alone, but you left me, and ran off, like someone had fired a gun up your…"

"There's my girls."

"Mum!" Debbie shouted, and ran towards her.

May hugged Debbie with one arm, and held another arm out to Jolie. "I've missed my girls."

Jolie embraced her aunt. "Welcome home, Auntie May." The smell of suntan lotion and alcohol reminded her of the holiday she, Debbie, and Molly had taken last year to Benidorm. The three of them running down the beach wearing long, curly blonde wigs, and red swimsuits, carrying bright orange, rescue floats.

The girls took a suitcase each, and walked over to the car park. May immediately began regaling them with tales of wild adventures on the high seas, which mostly involved avoiding a seventy-year-old randy grandpa for the two entire weeks' cruise, and a middle-aged couple who constantly bickered at each other, but insisted May shouldn't be on her own, and always saved her a place at their table.

As they approached the car, Peter got out, gave

May a hug, and took the cases from the girls. Debbie maneuvered Jolie towards the front passenger seat, telling her mum they would sit in the back, since she had news about her dad.

As the car moved off, May asked, "What's the news, then?"

Debbie grabbed hold of her mother's hands. "Dad will be home for Christmas."

Jolie looked over her shoulder. "Well, his parole hearing is on the fifteenth."

Debbie ignored her. "Isn't it fab?"

May lifted her hand, along with Debbie's, and kissed her on the knuckles. "It's nae guarantee, sweetheart. But, it would be wonderful to have yer dad home."

"We can have a big party for him." Debbie turned to Peter. "Speaking of parties, I've booked a meal for tomorrow night. You'll come, won't you, Peter? I've invited Alec."

"Yeah, sure, just tell me the time and place. I'm free. Like most nights," Peter said.

Aunt May's shoulders went back, and her brow creased. "Who's Alec?"

Debbie suddenly went all coy. Her cheeks had a rosy tint to them, and she cleared her throat. "It's Pete's friend."

"Oh, my god," Jolie laughed. "You *have* fallen for him, haven't you? You have never arranged a meal for us all before."

Debbie went stiff, and her jaw jutted out. "I like him, and yes, I want Mum to meet him." She eyed May. "And not at home, where the interrogation will be ten times worse. But, it's not that serious."

Jolie made kissing noises, then began to sing,

"Debbie and Alec sitting in a tree, k-i-s-s-i-n-g…"

"Oh, grow up. At least I can have a relationship with someone I like." Debbie nodded towards Peter.

Jolie took in a sharp breath. "I'm just messing." She turned to May. "Aunt May, do you know Molly's real dad, Bernie? Someone beat him up the other night, and he keeps looking at me like he wants something from me, or has something to say."

May's tanned face lost its colouring. She nervously touched her lips. "Why are you asking about him? He's a bit strange, well, mad really." She wiped at her brow. "Don't listen tae anything he says." She bent forward, and put her hand on Jolie's arm. "Stay away from him.

CHAPTER 9 OVERDRESSED

Jolie walked into Master Choo's Chinese restaurant on Sunset Road alone. Peter had arranged to take Alec, Aunt May, and Debbie to the restaurant.

The red carpet, cream walls, and mahogany tables appeared tired, but the ornate, brightly coloured paintings of women, fish, and birds brightened up the place. She closed her eyes at the sound of the tinkling traditional Chinese music. She sniffed, and caught the savoury aromas of sizzling food, and intoxicating spices. The atmosphere reminded her of a visit to Asia as a child with her mother.

Standing at the Great Wall, having her photo taken, her mother's red hair dancing in the wind. Another image was of a woman, with the blackest hair she had ever seen, wearing deep red lipstick and a bright blue robe, who sat playing a four-stringed, moon-shaped lute with a long straight neck. Her mother slowly pronouncing the name, Ruan.

Debbie's shrill voice brought her back to the present, and left her with an ache in her heart.

"Oh, my god. You have to help me. Mum is trying to act all posh around Alec. She is even calling me *Deborah*."

"Why would she do that?"

A little crease appeared on Debbie's forehead "Peter let it slip that Alec's grandad is a lord, I mean, a *real* lord. Viscount somebody, or other. Honestly, I couldn't get out of the car quick enough. I knew she would go all crazy." She glanced over her shoulder, and sighed. "Look at her," She turned her head back to Jolie. "She's fanning herself with that cheap plastic fan you got her from Spain."

Jolie moved her head to the side, and put her hand on her forehead. "The inhumanity of it all."

"Stop taking the mickey." Debbie grabbed Jolie's arm, and brought it down to her side.

Jolie yanked her arm back.

"She's acting like a teenager with a schoolgirl crush. Have you seen what she's wearing? That dress is way too short for her." She glanced up at the ceiling, exhaling slowly. "Lord, give me strength."

Jolie bit her bottom lip to suppress a giggle. She tugged at the hem of Debbie's skin-tight, short, woollen dress. "And this covers everything? If you bend over, we'll see what colour bra you're wearing, never mind your knickers."

Debbie pursed her lips. "I'm not nearly fifty, and it's not shocking pink. She looks like mutton dressed as lamb."

The girls walked over to the table, as May closed the fan, and wrapped both hands around it.

Alec stood up, and smiled at Jolie. He appeared handsome in a dark suit and tie, and crisp white shirt. Jolie looked him over. "He is pretty hot."

Debbie sighed. "Don't you start."

Alec glanced up, watching Debbie approach, his grey eyes sparkled, and the edges of his lips curled up.

May sat up straight, shoulders back, and chest out, her head held high. "So, Alexander, darling. I never asked you what is it you do?"

"Your daughter," he replied, his face emotionless.

Jolie covered her mouth, and burst out laughing.

May glared at him. "Well, really…" She fanned

herself again.

Debbie put her hands on her hips, and raised an eyebrow. "Now, will you behave yourself, and stop putting on airs and graces we all know you don't have?"

May's face reddened. "I didn't want him tae think we were commoners."

Debbie huffed. "We *are* commoners!" She shook her head. "We're working class, and proud of it."

May went to speak, but Jolie interrupted, "Let's look at the menu."

"Miss Bossy Boots Debbie," Alec planted a kiss on her cheek, "has ordered the set meal for us."

"I wasn't being bossy! Everyone agreed to the set meal when I asked," Debbie said.

"Yeah, sorry, I forgot. There's usually a good choice. Where's Peter?" Jolie asked Debbie

"Speak of the devil."

"Sorry, I had to pick my mother up from the beauticians." Peter sauntered up to the table, his yellow polo shirt showing off his broad shoulders. "She had this makeup, eyeliner thing tattooed on her eyes." He drew circles with his fingers around his eyelids. "They've swollen up that much. She couldn't drive."

"Is she okay?" Jolie asked, and took hold of Peter's hand.

Peter shrugged his shoulders. "She looks like she's been in the ring with Mike Tyson."

Jolie gasped.

"She'll be okay. She settled down, with a brew and an ice pack."

"I'll pop in, and see her after the meal," Jolie said.

Peter smiled at her. "She'll like that. She just said

the other day she hadn't seen you for a while."

"We'll get the drinks," Alec said, as he eyed Peter. "Come on mate, get your wallet out. Give those moths some exercise." He laughed.

"We still have the wine, we're fine," Debbie said.

Peter gave Jolie's hand a gentle squeeze, before letting go. "What do you want to drink?"

She clenched her hand, feeling the loss of his contact. "I'm driving. Sparkling water, please."

Jolie turned around, and Debbie was already seated next to May. She joined them at the table.

May's jaw went tense. "I saw that good-for-nothing ex of yers today."

"I seem to be seeing him everywhere, at the moment. I catch sight of him out of the corner of my eye, then, when I turn around, he's not there." Jolie rubbed her forehead. "I think I'm losing the plot."

May and Debbie exchanged a worried look. "When, and where, is this happening?" Debbie asked.

"Everywhere I go. Tonight, for instance, as I started the car to come here, I thought I saw him in the rear-view mirror. But, when I turned around, the street was empty." The hairs on Jolie's bare arms stood on end.

May tutted, and shook her head. "Start keeping notes of every time ye see him."

Jolie's stomach turned over. "Do you think…he's following me?"

"No, no, of course nae," May said. "I don't want you tae worry; it's just a precaution." She raised her left eyebrow, and grinned. "If he is, I'll be having words with him."

Peter brought the bottle of water over, and put it on the table, along with a tall glass containing a slice of lemon. "I'll be at the bar. Alec is in need of some man talk."

"Man talk," Jolie laughed.

Peter winked at her. "It's like girl talk, but with less shoes and handbags."

Jolie giggled, and watched him walk away. She jumped as May patted her arm. "Sorry, what?"

"I was just telling Debbie her dad called," May said. She sat back and the top of her dress slipped down, showing off her lacy cream bra. May quickly pulled the dress back up.

Shaking her head, Debbie grabbed the white lace shawl from the back of the chair. "Oh, for goodness sake, Mother. Put this on!"

"It is a wee bit tight." May said, grabbing the top of the dress, and twisting it from side-to-side. "I was in my twenties the last time I wore this, and flat-chested then."

The bottle hissed, as Jolie twisted the metal top off, and poured the fizzing water into the glass. "You look great, Aunt May."

Debbie huffed. "She looks like she hangs about in the red-light district of Amsterdam."

May slammed her hand down on the table. "That's enough, young lady. I might have gone a bit O-T-T, but don't ye dare speak like that about me. Do ye hear?"

Debbie's face flushed. "I'm sorry, I don't know what's wrong with me." Tears welled up in her eyes.

"Oh, darling, it's okay, dinnae greet," May said, and wrapped her arms around Debbie.

A thin, olive-skinned waiter, in his late teens, came out of nowhere, appearing at the side of the table. "Good evening, I place food, yes?" he asked in broken English.

"Yes, please," Jolie said.

He set down a large platter in the centre with barbecued ribs, chicken pieces on skewers, chicken wings, garlic mushrooms, and crispy fried seaweed. Then, he asked if they wanted soup.

"What type of soup is it?" Jolie asked.

"Chicken an' sweetcorn," he said.

May and Debbie said yes.

"Me, too, but we have two more with us." Jolie held up two fingers. "I'll go and ask them."

Just before she rounded the corner, voices drifted to her.

"You should ask her out. Tell her how you feel about her," Alec said.

"She doesn't think about me that way," Peter replied.

Jolie felt a pang of hurt. She had to remind herself they were just friends. He didn't think about her that way, and she shouldn't think that way about him. She took a deep breath and smiled. "Who doesn't think about you that way?"

Peter looked down at the bar. His Adam's apple bobbed up and down, and he wiped his brow with the back of his hand. "You don't know her... she's a client."

The smile left Jolie's face. *Of course she is. I bet she's beautiful and thin, and unbroken.* "You're gorgeous. Any girl would be lucky to be with you."

"See, she thinks you are gorgeous."

She watched, as Peter glared at Alec.

Am I staring? Do I look like I'm upset? "I'm not prying, but the food's here, and the waiter wants to know if you want soup?"

Peter picked his pint of beer off the bar, and walked off towards the table.

Jolie felt puzzled by his actions, and turned to Alec. "What's up with him? Did I say something wrong?"

"No, darling girl, you didn't. Its hormones, I think he's men-strating," Alec said, and laughed at his own joke.

Jolie groaned, and shook her head. "You are depriving some poor village of its idiot."

He linked his arm around Jolie's, as they head towards the table. Jolie tensed at the contact, and held her breath.

"Are you okay?" he asked.

She nodded, and tried to calm her beating heart with a few deep breaths.

"Debbie explained about…your past. You do not need to worry about me."

Jolie ground her teeth together. "She had no right!"

He raised his left eyebrow, and cocked his head to the side. "Hey, I don't judge, and she meant no harm. I'm the hero type, double-o-seven."

Jolie slipped her arm out of his. "Your arse must be jealous of the amount of shit that comes out of your mouth."

"You have to stop living in that great Egyptian river…de-Nile." He circled the air with his hand. "We both know I'm irresistible. And, let's not forget how hot I look."

Jolie's face flushed. *Oh crap. He heard me tell Debbie he was looking hot.*

As they reached the table, Jolie took a seat in between May and Peter, while Alec sat down next to

Debbie.

Placing her hand on Peter's arm, she asked, "Is everything alright?"

Peter smiled. "Yeah, just got some things on my mind."

"Me, too." She glanced sideways at Debbie.

"This soup is a bit bland," Alec said.

Jolie watched Alec, as he took another sip from the small white bowl with the lemon slice in it. "You're taking the mick, aren't you?"

Alec placed the bowl on the table, his brow furrowing, as he looked at them all laughing. "What?"

"That's the finger bowl, double-o-seven," Jolie said.

"Finger bowl? But, it's got lemon in it, I thought it was clear soup?"

May put her hand on her chest, and stifled a laugh. "It's for rinsing your fingers after eating the ribs."

"So, now you know." Alec cover his face with his hands. "I'm a Chinese virgin. Please, be gentle." He lowered his hands, and grinned. "Now, if it had been Indian, or Italian…" He slowly licked his lips.

"I can do both," Debbie said. She stared into his eyes, her finger lingering on the edge of her mouth. "Pizza, Chicken curry, onion bhaji …"

"Get a room! We are trying to eat here," Peter said, as he mimicked putting a finger down his throat.

The group was finishing the meal when Peter's phone rang. He excused himself, and walked away.

The waiter came over. "Was everything okay?" They all nodded, and agreed the food was good. "You want dessert? Coffee?" He asked.

"I couldn't eat another thing," Jolie said.

Debbie and May wanted ice cream, and Alec asked

for a coffee.

As the waiter left, Peter arrived back at the table. He took his wallet out of his back pocket. "I'm going to take off. Mum isn't so good. She's been on the phone to the beautician, and wants me to pick her some stuff up from the shop. How much do I owe?"

"Alec's already paid for the food," Debbie said, and put her arm around his shoulders. "I'll pay for the few drinks we've had."

"You're not driving, are you? You've had at least three pints and that whiskey," Jolie said. "I'll take you. I can pick you up in the morning to get your car." She glanced from May to Debbie. "I can come back for you."

Debbie waved her mobile phone in the air. "Don't be silly. Taxi will be ordered in a flash."

Peter grinned. "You don't mind?"

"No, course not," Jolie said.

"Yeah, cheers, mate," Peter said, and held his hand out towards Debbie with two twenty-pound notes. "Let me pay for the drinks. And if it's any more than that, let me know?"

Debbie took the money from him. "Thanks."

Alec kissed Debbie on the cheek, then looked at Jolie. "Can I grab a lift with you guys?"

"Sure," she replied.

May grabbed Alec in a bear hug, "Promise me ye won't be a stranger?"

Debbie sighed loudly.

Jolie laughed, and embraced May when she let go of Alec. "See you soon."

May leaned back, and ran her hand down Jolie's hair. "Drive safely."

Jolie gave Debbie a hug, and heard May telling

Peter to take care of his mum.

"I'll stop at the shop on Rover street; it's open twenty-four-hours now," Jolie said, and started the car.

When the entered the large store, Jolie headed to the magazine rack, and the boys walked off down one of the aisles.

Alec and Peter were standing next to each other in the check-out line, when Jolie caught up to them, noticing some funny looks from the spotty-faced male clerk as she did.

She stifled a giggle when she saw Peter and Alec were buying nothing but a large cucumber and a tub of Vaseline.

Suddenly, Peter's eyes widened in horror, and he blurted out, "No, we're just friends!"

The clerk moved back, his mouth contorted.

An old man tutted.

A middle-aged woman dragged her toddler close, and glared at Peter and Alec.

Peter's face turned beetroot red.

Jolie had to go wait in the car to stop herself from crying with laughter.

CHAPTER 10 BLIND DATE

Jolie paced around her living room, as she spoke into her mobile phone. "Er, sure, text me the address."

"Who's that?" Debbie mouthed from the leather comfy chair.

Jolie ended the call, and glared at Debbie. "That was Matthew. I can't believe you gave him my number!"

She shook her head. "No, I gave the number to my boss."

Jolie felt like steam would whistle out of her ears. "Why? Why would you do that, when it's pretty obvious she would give the number to her brother?"

Debbie waved Jolie off. "Matthew's harmless; the family's very religious."

"What?" Jolie picked up one of the cream cushions of the sofa, and threw it at Debbie. "And when were you going to tell me that?"

"Well, I don't know him, as such, but his sister is, and she said the family are great believers…"

Jolie threw another cushion at her. "You said he was sweet! I thought you knew him, or, at the very least, you had met him. You said you were at her house when you both came up with the blind date idea."

The cushion bounced off Debbie's arm. "Calm down, woman. She doesn't live with her brother. Hey, you never know, he might be a bit of a rebel, and will make you pray for forgiveness after he ravishes you."

"There's not going to be any ravishing."

Debbie opened her mouth, and Jolie held up the last of the cushions.

"If he starts preaching, I swear to god…"

"There you go. You're getting it already." Debbie shook her hands in the air. "Hallelujah." But, on seeing Jolie move forward, Debbie curled into a ball. Just in time, too, as Jolie whacked the final cushion against her shoulder.

Tears of laughter streamed down Debbie's face. "Okay, okay. I surrender. What did he want?"

Jolie looked deflated. "I've got to go and pick him up; his car's in the garage."

Debbie raised her eyebrow. "Please, don't tell me you are going dressed like that?"

Jolie inspected her knee-length dress and black ballet pumps, twirling around. "What's wrong with it? It's very flattering."

"If you say so, but baby blue doesn't exactly say I'm gagging for it."

"Well, there's a plus point. Look where your outfit got me last time." Her phone pinged, as a new message came in. She slid her finger across the screen, and opened up the message. "He lives in Carrwood, Hale Barns."

"I knew my boss was posh, but bloody hell," Debbie said.

"I drove through it once. You can't buy a house for less than a million pounds."

"At least it's not far. It's like twelve miles away." Debbie stood up, and walked towards Jolie.

Jolie threw her phone on the couch, and slumped down next to it. She put her head in her hands. *This is out of my league.*

Debbie sat down next to her, and put her arm over her shoulders.

Her phone pinged again. She took a deep breath, picked the phone up, and frowned. "Could I leave now, as he's made reservations?"

"Ooh la, la, lucky you. He's the dominant kind."

Jolie drove her little red compact car up to a large set of metal gates, tall red brick walls flanking it on either side. Her mouth fell open, when she rolled down the window to press the buzzer. "It's a friggin mansion."

She jumped at the loud buzzer, as a young male voice came through the intercom. "Come straight up to the house."

The gates swung open. Immaculate lawns guided the pebbled driveway to the large Edwardian house.

Jolie stepped out of the car, and squinted, as the sun bounced off the whitewashed walls. *I wonder how many rooms it has,* she thought. She started to count the windows and got to seventeen, when a tall, thin man in his twenties opened the double front door.

Jolie waved; he waved back, and walked out onto the porch. He looked over his shoulder, and the doors closed.

"Jolie?" he asked, and walked over to her with a beaming smile.

"Yes." Jolie held her hand out.

He bowed at the waist, and kissed the top of her knuckles.

"Matthew Montgomery-Brown, the third." He stood, and swooped his hand towards her car. "Shall we?"

Jolie's mind went blank. "Shall we what?"

"Shall we go, silly," he laughed gently.

"Oh, yes, of course. Pardon me." She giggled. "That was frightfully stupid." *Urgh, did I* really *just try and act posh?*

Matthew opened the driver's door for her.

"Thank you, kind sir," she said, and flicked her hair back over her shoulder with her fingers. *What is wrong with me? Get a grip, girl.*

"My pleasure," he replied, and headed around the other side of the car.

Jolie looked down at her market-stall clothes. *Oh, crap. I bet he drives a Bentley or a Porsche, maybe a Ferrari.* Her hand caressed the dints and scratches on the door frame, as she got in the car. "Where are we going?"

"I've booked us a table at La Mann's. I do love French cuisine, don't you?"

Double crap. Do I look like I dine at that kind of place? "Oh yes, nothing can compare to the food at La Mann's."

Matthew clasped his hands in front of himself, and smiled. "Oh good. One often gets stuck with philistines."

She bit the inside of her cheek, as she started the engine. *This is going to be fun.*

As they drove down the road, Jolie's phone rang. She pulled into a layby. "Sorry," she said, and grabbed the phone from the dash. "Hello?"

"Jolie."

"Hi, Peter, what's up?"

"I was wondering if you wanted to go for a drink?"

Jolie glanced at Matthew from the corner of her eye. "I'm a bit busy. I'm on a date."

Matthew winked at her.

She turned away, and looked out of the driver's window. The phone went quiet. "Peter, you still there?"

"Yeah, sorry. Enjoy your night." The phone went dead. She stared at it in confusion. *That was weird, not even a goodbye?*

"Was that your fancy man?" Matthew asked, with a sneer.

Jolie narrowed her eyes at him. "No!" She placed the phone back on the dash, and started the engine.

***

The metal bell at the top of the door tinged when they walked into the restaurant. A man in a dark suit and tie, with a large round belly, smiled at Matthew, then looked down his nose at Jolie.

She shifted from one foot to the other, and stared down at the floor.

"Good afternoon, sir, mademoiselle," he said.

"I have a reservation, Matthew Montgomery-Brown, the third," he said.

"Of course, sir. If you would follow me."

Jolie looked up, Matthew grabbed her hand, and they followed the maître d' into the dining area.

Wow, she thought, as she saw the three large, ornate, globe-shaped chandeliers dazzle in the centre of the ceiling. The plain white walls, with large paintings of single poppies and cream carpet, made the place feel cold and uninviting.

They stopped at a table in the far corner of the room. The maître d' pulled out a wooden chair, with a cream leather seat, for her.

The chairs look cheap. I've been in transport cafés that looked more expensive, and better quality than this. My nanna had furniture like this. Jolie realized she was being cynical, and made herself stop.

The maître d' pushed her chair in when she sat down. "Your waiter will be Kingsley. I'll send him straight over." He handed them each a menu and wine list, bowed his head, and walked away.

"It's quite small isn't it, just big enough for maybe thirty diners? You'd think a Michelin star restaurant would be bigger," Jolie said.

Matthew scowled. "I thought you said you had been here before?"

She felt her cheeks flush, and opened the wine menu to hide her face. "It was a long time ago. I got mixed up with which restaurant it was."

"Easy mistake. Which one did you think it was?"

"The one in Deansgate."

Matthew laughed. "That dump. This is a very different dining experience."

Crap car, cheap clothes, and now, he knows I lied about eating here. I'm going to die. Think of something else to talk about. "That's a huge house you have. Do you have roommates, or do you live alone?"

"My brothers and sisters are my roommates." He looked down at the menu.

"Oh. That's great you're so close…" A realization hit her. "Do you still live with your parents?"

He continued to read the menu. "Yes, and I'm not planning on moving out anytime soon."

Well, that's a turn off. "What's wrong with your car?"

He glanced up from the menu. "It's not really my car, it's Daddy's."

You've never had to work for anything in your life, have you? Jolie thought. *Why the hell was I embarrassed by my clothes and car? I've got nothing to feel ashamed of. I earn my money.*

"Now, we have established you are not used to this sort of dining, so don't worry. I'll order for us both." He flipped to the next page in the menu. "It's not cheap, but I'm paying, so don't you worry your pretty little head about that. You just sit there looking good."

How dare you? Condescending prick. She smiled her best I've-got-your-number-buddy type of smile, and picked up the wine list.

Pinot Noir, Dom. Du chevalier 2009 (£165).

Ooh, a nice Chardonnay

Dom. Louis Latour 2007 (£185)

An olive-skinned man approached the table. Jolie noticed the spark of anger in his dark eyes, which went as quickly as it appeared when he looked at Matthew.

His right leg slightly bent at the knee, his hips leaned to the left, he placed his right palm on his hip, and pouted. "Good afternoon. I'm your waiter, Kingsley, are you ready to order?"

Matthew's lips twitched, as he looked the waiter up and down. "Well, hello again, Kingsley. We'll start with the six course… taster menu."

The waiter narrowed his eyes. "Very good, sir, and what would you like to drink?"

Matthew opened his mouth to speak, but Jolie cut him off.

"Would you prefer a lovely Pinot Noir, Dom. Du chevalier 2009? Or they have a wonderful Chardonnay, Dom. Louis Latour 2007?"

Matthew swallowed loudly, and looked down at the wine list.

"We could get a bottle of each, if you're not sure?" She fluttered eyelashes at him, as he looked up.

"Chardonnay," he stuttered.

Jolie looked at the waiter, and grinned. "We'll have the Dom. Louis Latour 2007, please."

"Excellent choice, mademoiselle." The waiter cocked his head to the side, and smiled at her. He picked the wine menu up, and walked away from the table; his hips swayed about like he was trying to hula-hoop.

She placed her elbows on the table, and locked her fingers together. "So, I know your sister works as the manager at Darlington's, what is it you do?"

"As little as possible," he said, and took his mobile phone out. "Sorry, just have to send a quick text."

The waiter arrived with the wine. He poured a little into a glass, and waited for Matthew to taste it. Matthew picked up the glass, sipped at the liquid, then nodded, and held the glass out to the waiter.

Kingsley took hold of the glass, and Jolie watched Matthew deliberately run his little finger over the back of the waiter's hand. Kingsley jerked his hand back.

Jolie coughed, covered her mouth, and turned her head away. *This is great. I'm on a date with a pretentious snob, who is gay, and thinks he can belittle me. I was better off with Carl the Greek.*

"My sister tells me you're an orphan, and your mother was murdered?" He put the wine bottle back down in the centre of the table.

I'm going to kill Debbie when I get home. Jolie balled her hands into fists. *Stay calm. Remember, he's a prick.*

"You saw it happen, didn't you?"

Her throat dried up, and her nails cut into her palms. "Yes, my mother was murdered. Am I an orphan? Maybe. I have no idea if my father is dead or alive. Now, can we talk about something else?"

He lifted his wine glass to his mouth. "Do you not see Daddy then?"

Jolie could feel the muscles in her jaw twitch. "Does your family know you're gay?"

Matthew shot forward, as he began to choke on a mouth full of wine. Jolie cocked her head to the side, and raised an eyebrow at him.

The coughing subsided, and he repeatedly blinked. "I'm not gay. Whatever gave you that idea? Really, gay, indeed."

And I'm the queen of England. "There are things people don't like talking about; we all have skeletons. Shall we leave it at that, or do you have more intrusive questions about my past?"

He stammered, "Wh-what do you like to do for fun?"

Straight-faced, she said, "People watch."

Matthew started to fill her wine glass. "I was just having a bit of fun, before."

She picked her glass up, and held it out towards him. "To fun."

He clinked his glass on hers. "To fun."

The waiter arrived carrying a silver tray. He placed a long, narrow white ceramic board in front of Jolie. "Barbecued asparagus on baked chicken skins, with wild mushrooms."

Two pieces of asparagus on a bit of chicken skin. He's paying seventy-five quid for this crap. Idiot.

The waiter placed another ceramic board down in front of Matthew, and turned away from him. She noticed Matthew moved his elbow out to the side, and caught the waiter's bum. The waiter looked back, and smiled before leaving.

She stabbed a piece of asparagus with her fork. She could hear Matthew crunch on the skin and sighed, wanting to ask him to close his mouth as he ate. He had a double barrel name, lived in a mansion, but had the manners of a badly-behaved pig.

Neither of them spoke. Jolie continued to move her food around the plate throughout the awkward silence.

She cringed when Matthew belched loudly.

No sooner had he pushed his plate to the side than the waiter appeared with the second course. He served Jolie first again, and placed a grey slate platter down in front of her. "Venison with a blackberry glaze, rosemary-braised red cabbage, and wild garlic.

Jolie looked down. The amount of food on the platter would fit in the palm of her hand. She thanked the waiter, and looked across at Matthew, whose hand was resting on the waiter's arm, as he thanked him.

He quickly pulled his hand back, as he noticed her watching him, and stared at his plate.

She cut into a small corner of the meat, and gasped as blood seeped out onto her plate. *It's bloody raw.* She took a deep breath. *Just try it. Don't show yourself up.* She took a deep breath, and bit into the meat. The venison was slightly tougher than beef, and had a gamier taste. *Not too unpleasant, but I won't be in a hurry to have it again.* She nibbled away, in the uncomfortable silence.

Not able to cope with it any longer, Jolie asked, "I'm told your family is very religious?"

"My parents are Irish Roman Catholic," he said, revealing the half-eaten food in his mouth. He pushed the empty platter to the side.

She curled the left side of her mouth. *No wonder you*

haven't come out yet. "Are you religious? Do you go to church?"

"Only when they force me to. I'm the black sheep—the rebel." He winked at her.

Behind his head, the maître d' was showing three ladies to a table. One had curly red hair – her friend Molly.

"Oh my god, Jolie," Molly squealed with delight.

The maître d's head shot around, and gave her a disapproving look.

Molly said something to the two women, and hurried towards Jolie's table.

Jolie stood up, and walked towards her. "What are you doing here?"

"I'm with my boyfriend's sisters." Molly peered over her shoulder, and waved at the two women. "This place is lush. Glad I'm not paying. What are you doing here?"

Jolie tipped her head back, and sighed. "Debbie set me up on a blind date."

Molly stood on her tiptoes, her head bobbed up and down, as she tried to look over Jolie's shoulder. Finally, she learned to the side to look around Jolie, and her face paled. "Monty?"

Molly looked as if she was in shock. "You said you loved me? Why would you do this, and with my friend?"

Jolie closed her eyes. She wished the earth would open up, and swallow her. She felt Molly brush past her, and cringed at her trembling voice. She couldn't look at her friend, knowing the tears which would accompany it.

"I didn't know she was your friend," he said.

The blood pulsated in Jolie's her temples. "Really,

that's your answer? You didn't know we were friends?"

Molly burst into tears. She flung her arms around Jolie, and sobbed into her shoulder.

Matthew stood up, held his arms out towards the girls. "Mollykins."

Jolie ground her teeth together. "100,000 sperm, and the one that created your dumb arse was the fastest. Stay the hell away from her."

The two women who had arrived with Molly walked to Matthew's side. The oldest said, "Matthew, what is all this fuss about? Why are you here? And why is Molly upset?"

Jolie smirked, as she watched Matthew visibly shrink under the scrutiny of his sisters.

"Well?" the other sister demanded, arms crossed, lips pouted.

The maître d' came over, his head high, and eyes narrowed, as a result of the commotion. Looking down his nose at everyone, he said, "Please, you are upsetting the other customers. May I kindly ask you to take your seats, or leave the premises?"

The older sister turned around sharply, "You are new here, aren't you? My husband is Raoul La Mann, and if you ever speak to me like that again, I will have your job."

He went to speak.

She cut him off. "Go away."

The maître d' swallowed loudly, and waddled off with his head down.

The older sister turned her glare on Matthew. "What have you done?"

Matthew glanced at Jolie from the corner of his eye. The sisters looked at her confused.

"He's gay," Jolie said.

The room went silent. All eyes were on Matthew, whose face turned ashen.

Kingsley had made his way over, and stood to the side, just in view. He put his fingers to his lips, and blew a kiss in Jolie's direction, and mouthed, "Thank you."

Jolie turned away, but Molly slipped out of her grip.

Jolie grimaced when the loud slap echoed around the deathly quiet room. She wrapped her arm around Molly's shoulder. "Let's get you home."

Matthew held his reddened cheek in his hand, and sat down, his two sisters in front of him, arms folded. Jolie imagined them hitting him over the head with broomsticks.

"No, you go, Jolie." Molly glared at Matthew. "I haven't finished here yet."

Jolie looked around the room unsure, but Molly glanced her way, and nodded.

CHAPTER 11 OLD SCHOOL FRIEND

Jolie was face down on the cream carpet. "Found it," she said, and sneezed as she pulled a high heel from beneath Debbie's pink frilly bed. She sat up, and wiped the grey dust off the black patent leather with her palm. "You could keep pigs in here, if you cleaned it up a little."

"You cheeky cow. Nobody sees under the bed." Debbie said. She snatched the shoe from Jolie, and placed it on the floor next to its twin. Then, she opened the white wood doors to her wardrobe. The clothes hangers squealed along the rail, as she raked through her clothes.

Jolie sat down on the edge of the bed, and picked up a glossy magazine from the mirrored bedside cabinet, flipping through the pages. "Why do you buy these mags?" She turned another a page, and held it up. "Look, another picture of someone twerking. Their arse is bigger than my car. Seriously, what is it with big bums and twerking? And why are these people celebrities?"

Debbie turned around holding a short, low-cut red dress. "You are so uncool."

"Again, why do you buy this crap?" Jolie glanced back down at the magazine.

"So my cheapskate of a cousin can read them for free."

"Whatever. Who's the lucky guy?" Jolie flipped another page in the mag, and huffed.

"Alec."

Jolie's head shot up. "Again? That's a whole month now you haven't met up with anyone else?"

"Actually, six weeks since I started seeing Alec, and five weeks since I've seen anyone else."

Jolie's widened her mouth in mock shock, and put her hand under her jaw, pretending to force her mouth closed.

Debbie shook her head, and raised her eyes to the ceiling.

The doorbell chimed.

Debbie threw the dress towards the bed.

Jolie ducked, when it skimmed past her face. "Hey, watch it."

Debbie laughed, and headed towards the bedroom door. "If that's Alec's, I'm chucking you out."

"Charming."

Jolie closed her eyes when she saw Molly entering the bedroom. *Oh shit.* The bed dipped beside her.

"Hey," Molly said.

Jolie opened her eyes, and peered sheepishly at her. "I'm so sorry about last week."

Molly ran her hand down Jolie's hair. "You did nothing wrong."

"I'm still sorry for what happened."

Molly waved a brown-checked, Louis Vuitton handbag in the air. "Nothing to be sorry about. He keeps sending me gifts. I got this today."

Jolie scowled. "Nice. You've not taken him back, have you?"

"No." Molly grinned. "I keep telling him I don't want anything to do with him. But, he keeps sending me stuff, and begging me to take him back. His family believed you when you said he was gay."

Jolie shrugged. "It's true."

Debbie sat down on the chair by her dressing table. "Charlotte keeps apologizing at work, but she doesn't mention anything about him being gay."

"They are threatening to take him out of the will. He thinks if he has a girlfriend..." She cocked her head to the side, and raised her eyebrows.

Jolie huffed, and shook her head. "He'll still be gay."

"Let's all go out on the town tonight. My treat, or rather, Monty's. I just got two hundred quid for a set of diamond earrings he sent on Tuesday."

"Holy shit, he is desperate," Debbie said.

Molly glared at Debbie. "Hey!"

Jolie turned to Debbie, her eyes wide, jaw open.

Debbie rolled her eyes. "I didn't mean it like that."

Jolie turned back to Molly, "Debbie's got another date with Alec, and I'm just going to chill."

"Alec, again." Molly grinned. "Is he not getting a bit old and used for you by now?"

Debbie held her hands up above her head. "It's no big deal. It's not like we are getting married. We just enjoy each other's company."

Molly held her hands out in front of her, and made little jerking motions with her hips.

"Not everything is about sex," Debbie protested.

Jolie and Molly laughed.

Debbie stood up. "You two can be so childish."

"She has it bad," Molly said.

Jolie nodded. "Yep."

Molly grabbed Jolie's hand. "Lets you and me

paint the town red."

"Another night," Jolie replied.

Molly stuck out her bottom lip out. "Please, it's Friday night, and I'm all on my own." She cocked her head to the side, and fluttered her eyelashes. "The love of my life tried to cheat on me with one of my best friends."

Jolie's shoulders slumped. "Okay, but I'm not staying out late."

Molly wrapped her arms around Jolie. "Yay." She let go of Jolie, and leaned back, her eyes roaming up and down Jolie's body. "We better get you ready."

Jolie glanced at her black jeans and aqua-coloured long-sleeve shirt.

Molly raised an eyebrow. "You're not even wearing make-up."

Jolie brushed her cheek. "I've got tinted moisturizer and concealer on."

"That's exactly what I've been talking about," Debbie said.

Jolie held her hands out in front of her. "It's just a couple of drinks. I don't need to get dolled up."

An hour later, Jolie's hair was straightened, and her face delicately made up with pastel shades of pinks and browns. She reached for her handbag, and opened it up. "I've left my wallet at home, I'll be back in twenty minutes."

"I'll come with you. That way, we can just go straight out," Molly said.

The girls said their goodbyes.

They were halfway down the street, when Jolie notice figure dart behind the bus shelter. *I definitely saw you this time.* She rushed towards the bus stop.

"Hey, slow down," Molly called out, her voice a

little breathless.

Arms crossed, she ignored the pounding of her heart, and glared at Dave. "Have you been following me?"

Dave rubbed his hand over the stubble on his chin. She noticed the healing cuts on his knuckles, surrounded by old yellowing bruises.

"No, I...well—"

"I knew it. For weeks now, I thought I was going mad. What do you want?"

Molly gently took hold of her shaking hand, and gave her a reassuring smile.

He gripped the back of his neck. "Just to talk to you."

Molly stepped between them. "Weird way of showing it."

"It's okay, Molly. We're leaving." She saw the hurt in his eyes. *Why are you doing this?* She took a deep breath to steady her already frayed nerves, and walked away.

"You okay?" Molly asked.

Jolie nodded, afraid to speak, and let her voice betray how upset she really was.

The girls rounded the corner, and Molly gasped. "Isn't that the waiter?"

The slim, olive-skinned waiter from La Mann's waved his hands about like a man on fire, to get their attention. "Hi." He grabbed Jolie's rigid shoulders, and air kissed the side of her cheeks. He looked up to the sky, placed both hands over his heart. "I thought I was going to die. That piece of shit had been leading me on for over a year."

Jolie peeked at Molly from the corner of her eye.

He clasped his hands over his mouth, his eyes

darting back and forth. "Oh, it's you, I'm so sorry."

Molly waved him off. "Forget it. He's all yours."

He pouted, held his hand out to stop her speaking. "Bitch, please. I am so over that."

Jolie shook her head, and laughed. "This is Molly, and I'm Jolie..." She pointed at him. "Kingsley, right?"

He placed his hands at the side of his face, vogue style. "The one and only, darlings."

Two middle-aged men walked past, and Kingsley's gaze followed them, as they walked inside the Rose and Crown bar.

Kingsley pointed at the pub door. "Tell me you girls are going in there?"

Jolie shrugged her shoulders at Molly, who gave her a nod.

"Yeah, we can have a couple in here."

Kingsley put an arm through hers. "Honey, let me buy you a drink." He skipped to the door.

Jolie giggled, and grabbed Molly's hand.

They walked into the bar, the air vibrating with pulsating music. He let go of her arm, and started dancing his way to the bar.

"What are we having, girls?" He leaned over the bar, his bum sticking up in the air, glancing over his shoulder at them.

"Champagne," Molly shouted.

"Not while I'm paying."

"We all pay in the end, darling," Molly told him.

"We've got sparkling wine, four-fifty a glass, or twenty-five quid a bottle," the barman said.

Molly slammed fifty pounds down on the bar. "Three glasses and two bottles, please."

Kingsley turned to Jolie, and pointed towards

Molly. "I love this girl."

She explained the situation with Molly spending Monty's money.

"Well, I've seen who I'm taking home tonight." He licked his lips. "He keeps watching me, and before you ask, my gaydar has never let me down."

"How would he even know you're gay?"

"Hello!" He dramatically held out his arms, presenting himself, and twirled. The white hoodie tied around his slim waist fanned out.

"Go get him, tiger," Jolie laughed.

"Oh, honey," Kingsley explained, sticking his bum out. "This is the honey pot; the bear comes to me." He smacked his own backside. His arm caught a hairy-faced man next to him. He placed his hand on the scowling man's arm. "Sorry."

The man looked down at Kingsley's hand, and glared.

"Whoa, you work out," Kingsley gasped, then paused again. "Pity, I'm taken. But, you are gorgeous."

The man puffed his chest out, his reddened face turning almost purple. "Get your dirty faggot hands of me."

He jerked his hand away. "I'm sorry. It was just a joke."

Jolie edged up to Molly, her throat started to dry out. *Please don't fight.* Her legs felt like jelly.

"Your sort should be put down at birth," the man snarled, and spat on the floor next to Kingsley foot.

"What!?" Kingsley snapped. "Oh no, no way bitch," he said, waving his finger in the air. "I may talk like a puff, but I fight like a lesbian, so bring it on."

Hairy Face huffed, and stalked off.

Kingsley put one hand on his chest, and fanned his face with the other. "We girls don't need pigs like that. Phew, pass me that wine, sister."

Molly handed him a glass.

He downed the content in one gulp, and sat down next to Jolie. "Honey, you've gone really pale. Are you okay?"

She bit her bottom lip. "Yeah, I'm fine."

"I'll get another bottle of wine," Molly said.

"Shut the front door." Kingsley nudged Jolie. "That bloke is coming over, the one I had my eye on, before the Neanderthal got in the way."

Jolie took a deep breath. *I need to get out of here.* She squeezed her eyes shut.

"Play it cool. Tell him how sexy I am, really big me up."

Big you up? She opened her eyes, and a handsome, fair-haired young man was staring at her.

"Hi, Jolie."

Jolie tried to place his face. "Do I know you?" She swore her heart missed a beat, as she swam in his dark eyes.

"It's Laz, Lazarus Almsman." Dimples appeared on his cheeks, as he smiled.

Kingsley stood up, wiggled his shoulders, and held his hand out. "Kingsley, but you can call me anything you want."

Lazarus shook his hand, and turned back to Jolie. "You're looking great."

Kingsley flopped down on the chair, sighing. "Just my luck."

Lazarus… Oh my god, the spotty geek that never spoke to anyone. She pointed at him. "We had chemistry and maths together." Her eyes travelled up and down his toned body, well-fitting jeans, and tight t-shirt, showing off every contour. "You look amazing." She drew circles around her eyes with her finger. "Didn't you wear glasses?"

His grin widened. "Yeah, contacts now." He sat down opposite Kingsley. "I was pretty weird at school. Jolie was virtually the only one who spoke to me. She would say hi, as she passed me in class." A gentle smile crossed his face. "I never forgot that."

"You always seemed a bit lonely. I could relate," she said.

Molly came back with another two bottles of wine. Her jaw dropped when she caught sight of Lazarus.

"Molly, you remember Lazarus Almsman, from school?" Jolie said.

"Who?"

"Call me Laz."

Molly put the wine on the table, and held her hand out to him.

He ignored her, and picked up one of the Prosecco bottles. "You don't mind, do you?" He poured himself a glass.

Molly shrugged and squinted at him. "You do look familiar."

"Where's your boyfriend?" he asked Jolie.

"Single. And you?" Her face blushed.

"I don't have much luck with girls. I think they find me a bit neurotic." He downed the glass of wine in one.

Jolie glanced at Molly. Molly made circles with her finger at the side of her head.

We Can't Stop by Miley Cyrus came on. Kingsley jumped up, and grabbed Molly's hand. "We have to dance."

Molly giggled when he started twerking.

"Do you want to get dinner tomorrow night?" Laz said.

Jolie looked back at him. "Erm, yeah, sure."

"I'd better take your number," he said, and took out his phone.

Someone shouted over to Laz, he held his hand up, and waved. "Sorry, I've got to go." He topped his glass up. "I'll call you tomorrow. You choose the place."

Jolie nodded, and he headed towards the man who had called him.

Jolie was still getting over the shock, when Kingsley and Molly sat back down.

"Did you give him your number?" Molly asked.

Jolie nodded. Kingsley huffed, and called her a bitch.

Molly looked concerned. "He had loads of issues at school."

"People change," Jolie said, crossing her fingers.

"I hope so. He was so weird." Molly started laughing. "Remember when he wouldn't stop barking like a dog in English?"

"Oh, I forgot about that."

***

Jolie trolled the Internet, while talking to Debbie on the phone. "Okay, I want to keep the date casual, maybe just a meal in a bar, but somewhere not full of drunken idiots."

"I can't believe you got a date on your own, and it's with looney Laz."

"Don't call him that; that's horrible," Jolie protested.

She clicked on a link to a country bar, two miles outside of town. "Have you been to the Duck and Feather?"

"Yeah, it's nice, but really quiet."

"Perfect." Jolie opened the menu. "The meals are not a bad price."

"Well, at least I know where you are going…for when the police call round."

Jolie groaned. "I'm putting the phone down now."

"I'm serious. Keep me posted."

"Goodbye, Debbie." Jolie ended the call.

Her hair whipped about in the air like a whirly banshee, as the dryer blasted heat. In her peripheral vision, she caught the flash from her phone. Jolie didn't recognize the number. "Hello?"

"Jolie, it's Laz."

She smiled. "Hi."

"Are we still on for tonight, or are you going to bail on me? I am used to having girls bail on me."

"Wow, are you always this confident?" He didn't respond. "Err, of course we are still on. I found a lovely bar just outside town."

"I really want to go the Old Road, that new steakhouse in Market Square."

"Oh, okay." *Thought it was my choice.* "That's a bring your own bottle place, isn't it?" Again, she was met with silence. This is getting weird. "I'll bring a bottle of red."

"If you want. I'll be driving, text me your address."

Well, I'm certainly not going without alcohol now. "Okay. What time shall I be ready for?"

"Seven-thirty." The phone went dead.

She stared at the mobile is disbelief. "Wow. Should I bother with the lacey knickers and bra?"

Loud beeping from the street caught Jolie's attention. Laz waved at her out of the driver's window. She waved back, and clip-clopped in her stilettoes over to the fish tank, tapping on the glass. "Wish me luck, little guy. I think I'm going to need it." She took a deep breath, and smoothed down the front of her knee-length halter dress.

Laz ran around to her side of the car, and opened the door for her. Jolie took his hand, and her face warmed, as she thought about it touching other parts of her. *You are so friggin' hot, a bit weird, but hot.*

"You look pretty," he said.

Her face got hotter, as shyness gripped her. "Thanks." Her eyelashes seemed to take on a life of their own, as they fluttered. Forcing them to still, she focussed on the ground. "You look nice as well."

He patted his jacket and his jeans. "Oh no, I feel bad. I've forgotten my wallet, and if I go back for it, we'll miss our reservation."

Wait, what? What a scrooge. Then again, it could be a genuine mistake. "You can pay next time."

"You're a doll."

***

As they entered, Jolie blinked a few times to adjust to the poor lighting. Orange bulbs let off a subtle glow but not much else.

The waiter showed them to a table, and lit the triple candelabra. He placed the menus in front of them. "I'll get you some water and bread."

"Is it Perrier?" Laz said.

"I'll bring Perrier, sir, and for you, Miss?"

Jolie pulled the bottle of red wine from her oversized handbag.

"We have a five-pound corking fee."

"Fine," she sighed.

Laz opened the menu, humming as he scanned the page.

The waiter opened the wine, and poured Jolie a glass.

Laz excitedly announced, "Ohh, I think I'll have scallops for starters, and a fillet steak for mains."

Jolie opened the menu. Scallops (£15), fillet steak (£35). *You better be worth my while, mate.*

His finger gently caressed her wrist, then he fingered her gold bracelet. "I nearly bought myself a bracelet today, but couldn't. I don't like to spend money on a whim, so I deliberately leave it at home when I go out."

Her jaw moved back and forth, as she ground her teeth together. *So, you knew you didn't have your wallet on you? You are coming off less and less sexy by the minute.*

The waiter arrived with the water, and asked them if they were ready to order.

"We'll both have the scallops; we'll order the mains later." Jolie said, her tone a little sharper than she had meant it to be.

"Not sure what to have, pumpkin?" Laz said.

Pumpkin? Jolie's lips curled up at the edges. "Hmm." *We might not be here that long.*

Her irritation soared, as he drummed his fingers on the table. She tried desperately to think of something to say.

Her head shot forward. "What do you do for a living?"

A thin smile crossed his face. "I don't work. I'm on sickness benefit."

Her stomach dropped. "Oh, nothing serious, I hope?"

"I get freaked out easily, and have a lot of issues still. My medicine cabinet is like a chemist. I have anxiety and self-harm, when the stress gets really bad. I have lots of problems with my stomach, and shellfish and spices really upset it."

Jolie forced her mouth closed.

He continued, "I guess I shouldn't have ordered the scallops."

She looked up at the ceiling. *Why do you hate me?*

"I should be okay tonight; my new medication seems to be working."

The waiter interrupted with the starter.

***

"That was good," Laz said, and placed his cutlery on the plate. His stomach rumbled. "Oh no, I need the bathroom. Order me the fillet, if the waiter comes," he said, and made a dash towards the men's room.

The waiter came over, and topped her wine glass up. "Are you ready to order?"

She opened the menu. Fillet steak (£35) or rump (£18). Jolie smirked. "I'll have the chicken, and he'll have the rump steak please."

The waiting gave her a knowing look, and picked the empty plates up.

Time dragged, as she waited for him to return. Jolie checked her phone; ten minutes had gone by. She sent a picture message to Debbie of a woman swinging from a noose.

She searched Google for manic depressives. Sites popped up explaining it was now called bi-polar, which didn't make it any clearer.

The waiter returned again. "Would you like me to serve the mains now, or wait for your friend?"

She looked at her phone again. "He's been gone

over twenty minutes. Just serve it now, please."

The waiter bowed his head, and walked off, returning a minute later with the food.

Jolie jumped her phone vibrated in her hand. She opened up it to a picture from the film, *Texas Chain Saw Massacre*. She laughed and texted back.

I swear, I am flypaper for freaks. She gasped, as Laz suddenly appeared at her side.

"Sorry about that. I didn't mean to be so long," he said, and took his seat.

She couldn't read his expressionless face. "Is everything okay?"

His eyes dipped to table. "I have no illusions. I have issues, and I'm weird."

"We all have issues, and I'm not exactly normal. But, I'm going to be honest with you."

His face paled, and he opened his mouth, then seemed to change his mind about speaking.

She smiled at him. "I think you are hot. You are one of the hottest guys I have ever met. And I want to see what's under those clothes. But, you don't do yourself any favours." She twiddled her fingers. "I have confidence issues, but yours makes mine seem almost non-existent."

"Yeah, all that is true." He paused before blurting out. "I want to take you back to my place, and ravish you."

Jolie downed her glass of wine. "Ready when you are."

Butterflies fluttered in her stomach, when his smile reached his perfectly dark eyes.

***

The smell of greasy kababs and alcohol turned Jolie's stomach. She put her hands on her head to try and quiet the pounding, walking to the kitchen. Spencer darted back and forth in his tank. "Later, little guy. I'm going back to bed." The squeal from the tap vibrated through her body. She filled the glass with water, and went back to the bedroom. Gingerly, she lay down, popped two pain killers in her mouth, and closed her eyes.

Her eyes opened to the banging on the door. She groaned, and checked the time. She'd slept for a couple of hours.

She opened the door to Debbie.

"I want all the juicy details."

"I want coffee," Jolie said, and headed to the kitchen.

"Looking at the state of you, you must have had a good night," Debbie said.

"Oh god, I am so over men."

Debbie switched the kettle on. Jolie threw the half-eaten kabab in the bin, and placed the half-empty wine bottle in the fridge.

"Do me a favour. Feed Spencer. I can't face the smell this morning."

Debbie put the mugs of coffee on the small round table. "Morning? It's nearly lunch." She picked up Spencer's food, and slid the lid back. "You have such a bad mummy, Spencer. Aunty D will look after you."

Jolie put her head in her arms, and leaned on the table. "No men, and *definitely* no alcohol. I swear I'm going to turn into a lesbian." She cringed, as a chair scraped across the floor.

"Come on, what happened?"

Forcing herself to sit up, Jolie relayed the story of Laz having a problem with shellfish, and after eating scallops, farted continuously in the car back to his apartment, which turned out to be a bedsit. After getting over the shock, and her telling herself it was all nerves, not to judge, and she didn't want to fail at another date, they started getting it on, and slowly undressed each other. When they were both half-naked, he came in his underwear, and then insisted she leave while he called his doctor, because he was feeling too stressed to deal with anything. It was eleven p.m., and he was in such a state, she couldn't get the address from him to call for a taxi.

Debbie laughed so much, the tears were running down her face. "You are right. Your only hope is to become a lesbo." Her phone beeped. "It's Alec. I'll pop back later. You get yourself back off to bed for an hour; you look like shit."

She kissed Jolie on the back of the head, and left.

Jolie dragged herself to the couch, and wrapped a blanket around herself.

***

The next morning Jolie's eyes sprung open, when she heard banging on the door.

"Hold your horses, I'm coming," she shouted. She opened the front door. Debbie stood in the hallway. Jolie's stomach dropped at the sight of her pale complexion and red eyes. "What's happened?"

Debbie trembled. "Can we sit down?"

Fear gripped her. "Yeah." She watched Debbie, as she hugged herself, and slowly made her way inside.

Jolie sat next to her, and wrapped her arms around her. "What's wrong? You're scaring me." She desperately tried to keep control of her emotions.

"Alec found a lump in my breast." She took in a shaky breath. "Grandma died from breast cancer."

CHAPTER 12 THE LUMP

"Are the wicked witch and Harold back yet?" Peter asked.

Jolie giggled. "No, but they shouldn't be long. Can I pass a message along?"

Peter slipped on his dark grey jacket. "No, I'll catch him when I get back. Maybe text me when he gets in."

"Sure." The phone rang. "Jones, McCarthy, and Day."

"Jolie."

She mouthed to Peter, "Sorry, it's Debbie." Then, she turned her attention back to the phone. "Did you get a doctor's appointment?"

Peter took a step forward, his face full of concern.

"They got me straight in," Debbie said.

Jolie closed her eyes. "I wanted to come with you. What did they say?"

"Alec came with me. The doctor agreed; there is a lump."

"Oh," Jolie said, her lip trembled.

Peter took hold of her hand. "What did they say?"

She put her other hand over the mouthpiece. "Alec was right."

"I have to wait for a hospital appointment. The doctor assured me these things are dealt with very quickly," Debbie said.

"What's very quickly? A day? A week? A month?"

Jolie asked, and squeezed Peter's fingers.

"I don't know, but Alec is going to speak with his mother about a private doctor. I'll come and see you tonight. I'm really scared."

Jolie looked pleading at Peter. "Give me twenty; I'll get a couple of hours off."

Peter nodded in agreement.

"No, I'm just off to see Alec's mother. I'll come see you tonight."

"Okay, I love you." Jolie put the phone down, and let out the sob she had been holding back.

***

The bright lights bounced off the white walls, the smell of disinfectant heavy in the air. Jolie picked up a magazine, and the chair squeaked, echoing in the silence. Her mind raced, as she tried to think of something reassuring. Nothing. She had to speak, say something, anything. "I thought it would be different, these private hospitals, but it reminds me of our NHS ones."

"It is a National Health hospital, it's just the doctor that's private. But, it's amazing what having money and a title can do. I'd probably be waiting a month, rather than the week it took Alec's mother to get me in with her doctor," Debbie said, a slight tremor audible in her voice.

Jolie's heart thumped in her chest every time a nurse entered the waiting room. She didn't know what was worse, the fact a nurse was coming for Debbie, or the fact they didn't call her. The waiting played on her nerves. She pulled at the collar of her cream, roll-neck jumper. "It's hot in here." She slipped her jacket off.

"Debbie Rayford," a young nurse called out.

Debbie's legs trembled when she stood.

Jolie stood up with her, and squeezed her hand. "I'm right here."

"Do you want your friend to come with you?" A delicate smile formed on the nurse's lips. She almost looked angelic.

"Yes, I don't want to go in on my own."

Their footsteps reverberated, as they followed the nurse down the long stark corridor into a small cubical.

The nurse handed Debbie a blue hospital gown. "Strip down to the waist, and put this on. Doctor won't be long." She smiled reassuringly.

The nurse left, allowing Debbie to change.

"No selfies. I know I look hot," Debbie joked when she emerged from behind the screen.

Jolie rolled her eyes. "So hot."

The Doctor entered. "Hello, Miss Rayford, I'm Doctor Stewart." The cheesiest grin crossed his aging face. He reminded Jolie of a used car salesman.

The Doctor held his hand out, and Debbie shook it.

He glanced at Jolie. "Who do we have with us?"

"My cousin, Jolie," Debbie said.

He took Jolie's hand, giving it a firm shake. "Wonderful of you to come and give support." He turned his attention to Debbie. "So, you found a lump?"

Jolie's stomach did somersaults and her mouth began to dry up, as Debbie spoke.

"Yes, on my left…" Debbie touched her breast.

"Any pain?"

She nodded.

"Okay. Do you mind if I examine both breasts?"

he asked.

"No, go ahead," she said, her face pale.

He looked from Jolie to Debbie. "Do you want to go behind the screen?"

Debbie nodded, and reached for Jolie's hand.

"I know this is scary, so if you have any questions, just ask. I'll examine the one with the lump first. Can you point to the area? And if at any time you feel uncomfortable, just let me know, and we'll stop." A reassuring smile lit up his face.

A cold sweat ran over Jolie's body.

"There are two small lumps. The best thing is to do a mammogram, a scan, and then, take a little sample by syringe." He sat down beside Debbie. "Do you have any questions?"

"No, not yet."

Jolie's bottom lip trembled. *Oh god, please, don't have cancer.* She wasn't allowed to go in the room where they did the mammogram. She paced the floor, waiting for Debbie to return.

Eventually, Debbie returned to the waiting area. Jolie took hold of her hand. "You've been ages, is everything alright?

"Just have to wait for the results," Debbie said.

"Was it as painful as people say it is?"

Debbie shook her head. "The mammogram is more uncomfortable than painful. They took samples from the lumps by syringe, and that hurt like a bitch." Fear crossed her delicate features. "They're testing it now."

Jolie choked back tears. "Everything will be fine."

Debbie placed her head on Jolie's shoulder. "I don't think so. I have this feeling... I can't explain it."

Debbie's hand shook in Jolie's. She heard the sniffle, as the tears wet her shoulder. Jolie desperately tried to hold it together, and clung on to Debbie. Her vision blurred when she tried to blink away the moisture.

Time dragged on. People came and went, most of them trying to avoid making eye contact.

The nurse came back, and called Debbie. The smile had gone from her face, replaced by an 'I'm-so-sorry' look.

Jolie was uncertain how to move, fearful her legs would not hold her upright. Debbie's nails dug into her palms when they neared the Doctor's room.

The Doctor's appearance was different. He looked more like a doctor, his face void of emotion, his voice calm and controlled.

"Please take a seat."

The girls sat down, and he pulled his chair close to Debbie. "We have to do another biopsy. We need to take more tissue, and it will just be a local anaesthetic. It takes a couple of hours for the results."

"Why?" Jolie asked.

"The results from the fine needle aspiration were inconclusive."

Debbie gave her hand a gentle squeeze. "I'll be fine. You go and wait in the waiting room."

Inconclusive? Jolie nodded, too afraid to speak.

Every step she took felt like she was abandoning Debbie, and closing the door was the final straw, she wanted to run, to scream, to kick out at something. Instead, she took a deep breath, and sat down on a cold plastic chair.

***

Debbie placed a cold chicken salad on the tray, and

Jolie ordered the lasagne. They took a table next to the window that looked out to the perfectly manicured garden.

Jolie lost her appetite, and after a few mouthfuls, she placed the fork on the plate.

"You need to eat," Debbie said.

Jolie looked over at Debbie's plate. Most of the chicken salad was untouched. "So do you."

Debbie reached for her bottle of water. "I've eaten a lot more than you have." She took a long drink.

Jolie looked at her watch. "God, we've only been gone twenty minutes." She sipped her cup of tea.

"Do you have a will?" Debbie asked.

Jolie banged her cup down on the table. "What the hell?"

"We did one at work; I wondered if you had one. And I've got to be realistic."

Jolie lowered her voice. "You are not going to die. You don't even know if it's cancer yet."

Debbie kept her eyes fixed on the table. "Yeah, I do."

Jolie couldn't think; she found it hard to take a breath. "I need some air."

"Me, too. Then, we can head back."

They put their trays in the racks, and went into the garden.

They stopped at a bench, and watched the small black and white wagtail birds feeding on insects too small for Jolie to make out.

Jolie cringed when Debbie spoke about the insurance she had taken out on the mortgage last year. And how she wanted Jolie to have all her jewellery and shoes. She couldn't help but laugh when Debbie told her there was no point in Jolie getting her clothes; she wouldn't get one tit into any of her blouses or tops.

"Cancer isn't always terminal," Jolie said, almost to herself.

"I know, but I want to be prepared for the worst, just in case."

They held each other in a quiet moment, which silently spoke of their love for each other, before heading back to await the results.

***

The Doctor was clear and concise as he explained to Debbie she had breast cancer, and they would attack it from two sides, surgery and chemotherapy. Jolie's mind shut off. Time seemed to stand still. She watched and heard everything going on, but nothing registered. The walls started to close in. She needed to escape, get fresh air.

Debbie stood, and shook the doctor's hand.

Jolie automatically stood up as well, and a cold sweat ran down her back.

The Doctor's mouth moved, as he frowned.

Debbie appeared in front of her. Jolie watched her speak, but the words made no sense.

Jolie shook her head, and tried to clear the fog. "What?"

"Bloody heck, you scared me then. You look grey," Debbie said.

"I'll get the nurse to bring some water; you've both had a bit of a shock," the Doctor said.

Jolie refused, and darted to the door on wobbly legs. "I just need fresh air."

She gulped great lungful of cool moist air, and sat down on the stone steps.

Ten minutes later, Debbie's warm hand brushed

against her cold arm. She handed over her jacket.

"I'm sorry. I didn't mean to freak out. I'm okay now. I won't let you down again." Jolie felt Debbie sit next to her.

"I was freaking out, too. When he asked if I had any questions, there were only two things I could think of that I wanted to know. Number one, am I going to die? And number two, will my hair fall out? To which he responded, 'No,' and 'yes.' It's took me over six years to get my hair to this length."

Jolie wiped the corner of her eye.

"I can't believe I'll be in hospital on Thursday. It all feels so…surreal. I've only got few days to sort everything out."

Unable to look at Debbie, Jolie focussed on a beetle scurrying about in front of her. "Are they going to take away your breast, then?"

"No, just some of the tissue."

"I was a total shit in there, and you must have been so scared."

"A little. But, I'm more scared of what it's going to do mum when I tell her." She sniffed. "Will you come with me?"

"Of course! You are not getting out of my sight. Ever!"

Debbie moved, and stood in front of Jolie. "Well, there's no time like the present. Let's go."

"Now?"

"Now. Mum will be home from work soon."

***

Jolie and Debbie sat on the couch, holding on to each other's hands, as May walked into the living room.

"Why do you two look like you have been up tae nae good?" Her brows knitted together. "Yer nae pregnant are ye?"

Debbie shook her head. "Sit down, Mum."

May turned her attention to Jolie. "You?"

"Mum, I've just come from the hospital."

May slumped down into her chair. They went to her side.

"Mum, I have cancer."

"What?" May shook her head. "That's not something you find out about just like that?"

"I found a lump, and I didn't want to worry you, in case it was nothing."

"You didn't want tae worry me?" May burst into tears.

Jolie and Debbie let their emotions get the better of them, as they tried to explain what had happened, and what was going to happen in the future.

CHAPTER 13 DESPERATION

Jolie's feet felt like they were weighed down, as she aimlessly wandered the corridors. She squinted under the bright fluorescent lighting, which, along with all the worry about Debbie, made her head pound.

She leaned her forehead on the cool, comforting glass. "Please be okay," she whispered.

The hairs on the back of Jolie's neck stood on end, when she felt someone watching her. Then, he called her name. Her muscles tightened. She turned, coming face-to-face with Dave. "What are you doing here?"

His brow creased. "I had an appointment. Never mind me, are you okay?"

She shuddered, and tears began to form, blurring her vision.

Dave stepped closer.

She wanted to back away, but had nowhere to go. Her bare arms touched the cold window.

He took hold of her hand.

It felt good—comforting.

She closed her eyes, the warm tears trickling down her face.

"It's Debbie," she whispered.

"I've heard."

She opened her eyes. "They're operating now. Aunt May's there…with Alec."

His hand tightened around hers. "Who's Alec?"

She withdrew her hand from his. "Her

boyfriend."

He stepped closer.

The warmth of his breath on her face, the smell of his aftershave, brought memories flooding back, of lying next to him, and feeling his flesh against hers.

She placed her hands on his chest, and pushed him away.

He took hold of her wrists. "I miss you." His forehead touched hers.

"Please, don't," she pleaded.

His lips brushed against hers. She leaned into the kiss.

He let go of her wrists, and wiped a tear away from her chin with his thumb. "If you need anything, I'll be here. I'll always be here." He stepped back.

Her lips prickled from the electrifying kiss. Jolie realized, at that moment, she had forgiven him, had stopped hating him for what he had done, and probably never hated him in the first place. However, she hated herself for it.

"I'm sorry," she whispered, and pushed past him.

She raced outside, the cool air a welcome relief. Automatically, her hand went to her cheek. She could still feel his hand.

Aunt May appeared in front of her. "She's out of surgery; it went well."

Jolie threw her arms around May, and hugged her.

"Come on, honey. Get yourself home, and get some sleep. I'll stay, and ye can come back tonight."

Jolie nodded, and let go of May. "Where's Alec?"

"He's staying." She smiled. "Such a nice laddie."

"Yeah." She gave May a kiss on the cheek, and went home.

Sleep didn't come easy; Jolie tossed and turned,

kept checking the time, but eventually, she dozed off for a couple of hours. When she woke, she still had an hour to go until visiting time, but she couldn't wait at home any longer. *Maybe they will let me in early?*

***

Jolie parked in the hospital car park. She checked the clock on the dashboard. 6:45pm. Visiting hours didn't start until 7:30pm. After watching the clock for ten minutes, she got out of the car, and walked towards the entrance. A crowd of around twenty-five people had begun to gather near the main doors. The crowd was mumbling, and staring up at the hospital roof.

Jolie squinted, and shielded her eyes, as she looked up at the figure on the ledge forty feet above the ground. She gasped. "Dave."

Dave stood on the edge on the roof, his hands gripped the thick iron guard railing, and his eyes were shut. He inched out, throwing a leg over the barrier.

Jolie shouted, "No!"

He swung the other leg over the rail.

"Dave, please. Don't do this!"

He opened his eyes, and glared at her.

Her body went cold. She put her hand over her mouth, shaking her head at him.

Dave looked behind himself. "Stay away."

Jolie got up on tip toes, straining her neck to try and see what he was looking at. She called out to him, "Dave, please."

Dave looked down at her, and two men grabbed his arms, and hauled him back.

Jolie raced inside. She ran up the stairs, taking them two at a time.

She spotted Dave coming down.

He was calm, flanked by the two security guards.

He spotted Jolie, and closed his eyes.

"Where are you taking him?"

***

Every time Jolie closed her eyes, she saw the haunting look on Dave's face, him telling her he'll call.

"Are you expecting a call?" Debbie asked.

"Hmm?" Jolie looked across at Debbie.

"Are you expecting a call?" Debbie nodded towards Jolie's phone. "You're checking it every five minutes."

Jolie shook her head. "No." She slipped the phone into her back pocket. *What the hell am I doing? I'm here for Debbie, not him.* "I'm sorry. How are you feeling?" She looked from the drain protruding out from Debbie's hospital gown, to the monitor and its continuous beeping.

Debbie scowled at her. "You already asked me that. What's going on?"

Jolie forced a smile, as Debbie, May, and Alec stared at her. "I'm asking again."

Debbie reached her hand out for Jolie's. "Are you sure you are okay?"

Jolie wrapped her hand around Debbie's, and rubbed the back of her knuckles with her thumb. "I'm fine. You're the one who's sick."

"I'm not sick."

"You have just had major surgery, and you look pale and in pain."

"I'm just a little groggy. My boob is a little sore, the drain to take away the fluid is a little uncomfortable, but it's not as bad as I thought it would be. To be honest, I just want to sleep."

Jolie gave her hand a quick squeeze, and nodded.

May stood up. "Okay, honey." She kissed Debbie

on the forehead. "Get some rest, and we will see ye tomorrow."

"I'll drop you at home, May," Alec said, and ran the back of his fingers across Debbie's face. "I'll see you in the morning." He kissed her on the lips.

Jolie waved goodbye, and left the hospital room.

May and Alec joined her in the corridor, and they all walked to the car park. Jolie made an excuse that she needed to go to the bathroom, and after saying goodbye, walked back into the hospital.

The front desk felt like an imposing, never-to-approach alien being. She watched people going up to the receptionist and asking questions, before turning away and leaving.

She squared her shoulders, and walked up to the woman with the stern face and pointy glasses. "Hi, I'm trying to find out where David Green is."

The woman clicked away on her keyboard. "When was he admitted?"

"Just over an hour ago."

The woman looked up over her glasses. "I don't have a David Green."

Jolie cleared her throat. "He was the man on the roof."

The woman's eyes narrowed. She clicked away at her keyboard again. "Ward four." She pointed at the exit doors with her pen. "Through the main doors, across the car park in the building opposite."

Jolie thanked her, and followed the directions to the other building.

She pulled on the door handle, but the door didn't budge. Her finger went towards the silver intercom and paused, afraid of what the touch could mean. She let out a slow steady breath, and pushed the buzzer.

"Ward four."

"I was hoping to see David Green. He's just been admitted."

"What's your name?"

"Jolie Winters."

She was met with silence. The seconds dragged on. *What if he's told them he doesn't want to see me? Is this my fault?* She bit her thumbnail.

Does he hate me? She stopped biting her nail, and ran her fingers through her hair. The car park was almost empty—no people about, no noise. She turned to leave, and a high-pitched buzzer sounded.

"Come to the top of the stairs, and we are right in front of you."

Each step felt like ten, and as the doors at the top came into view, her heart raced. Jolie's legs felt like they would buckle, and her mind went blank. All she could think was *run*.

Her hand trembled when she put it against the 'push' plate. When the door opened, a friendly looking nurse, with a warm smile, greeted her.

"Hi, Jolie?"

Jolie nodded.

The nurse pointed to a room on the right. "Dave's in there."

She walked in, and saw Dave sitting, talking with a doctor. Dave smiled at her.

The Doctor stood, and held his hand out. "May I call you Jolie?" He didn't wait for her answer. "I'm Doctor Jackson. I have just been explaining to your husband we won't be keeping him in."

She shot a look at Dave; he hung his head low.

The doctor continued, "He needs to make an appointment with his GP."

Confusion coursed through her. "Shouldn't he be sectioned? He tried to kill himself."

"We're here, if he needs us." He turned to Dave. "The nurse will be up with the medication soon, then you can go. Any problems, call the ward."

Opened-mouthed, Jolie watched the doctor leave. "I don't understand. You need to be somewhere safe!"

Dave shrugged his shoulders. "Cutbacks, I guess."

She scowled at him. "Why did he think I was your wife?"

"It was the only way they would let you in."

"What were you doing here in the first place? At the hospital, I mean."

He rubbed his hands together nervously. "Doctor Jackson is my psychiatrist. I've been seeing him for a while now."

She pinched the bridge of her nose. "Is this my fault?"

He grabbed hold of her shoulders. "No, why would you think that?"

She shrugged. "I don't know."

"I messed everything up. I lost you, my job. Now, my flat." A tear snaked down his cheek. "My family hasn't spoken to me in months. It all got to be too much. But, mostly...mostly, I missed you."

A lump formed in the back of her throat.

"I love you so much."

She backed away.

He shifted his eyes down to the floor. "I know I don't deserve you, or your forgiveness. I don't deserve anything. I don't have a reason to live."

She covered her mouth with her hand. "Don't say that. Don't *ever* say that."

He nearly collapsed onto the floor, dropping to his knees in despair. "I'm scared, babe. Really scared. I don't think I can carry on anymore. I have nothing, I *am* nothing."

Jolie rushed forward, and knelt down next to him. "You're not nothing." She wrapped her arms around him. Desperate to keep her emotions in control, she bit her lip.

"You were the only good thing to ever happen to me. You kept me sane." He drew her onto his lap, and nuzzled the side of her head.

Oh god, I need to go…I can't leave him like this.

"I missed you so much."

"I missed you, too."

His arms tightened around her. "Give me a reason—something to live for."

"I can't," she murmured.

He placed his hand at the back of her neck, and gently massaged. "We were so good together."

Her breathing quickened.

His forehead landed on hers. "I want to wake up with you in my arms. I want to make you happy."

"Please, don't."

The door opened, and a nurse walked in and coughed. Jolie jumped up. Dave stood up, and took hold of Jolie's hand.

The nurse smiled, and handed over the medication. "One tablet, twice a day. They may make you a little groggy."

"I don't have anywhere to go," he said.

The nurse scowled, and quickly regained her composure. "I can give you some numbers to local shelters."

"You can stay with me for a few days." The

moment the words left her lips, Jolie wanted to take them back.

Dave's face lit up, and he squeezed her hand.

She desperately wanted to jerk away, but had second thoughts, with the nurse still in the room.

"Good luck, Dave. You can call the ward, anytime," the nurse said, and gave Jolie a warm smile.

***

Jolie opened the door to her flat. Dave paused at the threshold.

"What's wrong?" Jolie asked.

"It's strange, being back here, with you."

A nervous laughed left her lips. "Yeah, it is."

Jolie walked in, stopped half way into the living room, and motioned her head for him to follow.

He looked around the living room, and smiled. "So many memories in here."

Jolie smiled. "I'll get the spare duvet and pillows for the couch." When she returned, she placed the bedding on the chair. "I need a drink."

"Me too," he said, and flopped down on the sofa.

Jolie grabbed two glasses, and a bottle of wine.

CHAPTER 14 MISTAKE

The pounding in her head woke her up. She groaned, and felt the warmth of another body. Her hand ran down his bare chest. "Oh shit."

"And good morning to you, too," Dave said.

Jolie sat up, and clutched her head. "I need pain killers."

"I'll get them, babe," he said, and dragged the sheet back.

What the hell have I done? She sat on the edge of the bed.

Dave handed her two pills and a glass of water. She thanked him, and took the pills.

"How, I mean, me and you…I don't remember a thing."

"I'm not surprised. You drank the majority of the three bottles of wine." He chuckled.

"Not so loud." She held her head in her hands.

"Back to bed with you." He gently took hold of her and laid her down, then got in beside her, and wrapped his arms around her.

A few hours later, Jolie woke up desperate for the toilet. She braced herself for the onslaught of pain as she got up. Dave murmured when she moved from his embrace.

When she returned from the bathroom, he sat up, the most wonderful smile on his face. It even reached his eyes. A shiver went through her, as she took in his perfectly toned chest and abs.

"Good morning, beautiful," he said, and lifted the sheet.

***

Jolie walked onto the ward. The familiar bright lights and smell of disinfectant greeted her. Debbie waved from the old metal hospital bed, with light blue covers on it.

Debbie's eyes wandered up and down Jolie's form. She reached out, and touched the rounded collar of the baby pink shirt. "Is this new?"

Jolie ran her hand down the front of the shirt. "Yeah, well, no. I got it a while ago, but never wore it."

Debbie frowned. "You look different, happier?"

She couldn't help the forming grin. "I'm happy. The most important person in the world to me is going to be okay."

"More like it's the extra two days you got off work." Debbie giggled.

Alec sat on the edge of the bed. "Tough as old boots, this one."

Debbie slapped him on the arm. "Don't compare me to a pair of smelly old boots."

Jolie laughed. "Yep, she's back to normal."

May walked in, her shapely hips causing her flowing dress to swing from side-to-side. A man visiting the woman opposite watched her every move.

"May, I think you have an admirer," Alec said, and indicated towards the balding man.

May flushed. "Oh, please. I'm a married woman." She took a second look over her shoulder.

"Mum!" Debbie protested.

May giggled. "It's just a bit of fun, honey. Anyway, I've spoken to the nurse, and she said if ye get the drain out today ye can come home in the morning."

Debbie huffed. "Didn't I tell you that when you came in earlier?"

May lifted her hands up in surrender.

"I told you the doctor said, if they take the drain out today, I will be able to go home tomorrow. Honestly, I don't know why I bother."

"Oh, I almost forgot." Jolie grinned, and she reached down for her oversized black and tan handbag. She withdrew a box of milk tray assorted chocolates, and handed them to Debbie. "Got you these."

"If you weren't family, I could fall in love with you." Debbie beamed.

Jolie pulled a face at her. "You are so weird. Stop with the lesbian jokes."

A nurse walked over to them. "I'm sorry, can I just ask you to leave for five minutes while the doctor comes and takes the drain out?"

Jolie and May paced the corridor, until the curtain was drawn back. They re-joined Debbie.

"Did it hurt?" Jolie inquired.

"Not really. It stung a little bit, because the drain has caused a blister, but it didn't hurt."

"I'll pick up some things from yer flat this afternoon," May said.

"Mum, I already told you, I'm going home, as in *my* flat. Alec is staying with me."

Jolie saw the hurt on May's face. "It wouldn't hurt, just for a couple of days."

They watched May wipe her eyes.

Debbie bent towards her mother. "Why don't you stay with me?"

May smiled. "I'd like that."

"I just want things to feel as normal as possible, you know?"

May wiped away the final escaping tear. "Of course ye do," she sniffed.

"Have they said when the chemotherapy will start?" Jolie asked.

"In about a month. I have to heal first."

Jolie's phone beeped, she swiped the screen to read the message. It was from Dave.

Are you going to be long? I love you.

I had better get back; I don't want to upset him while he's ill. **No, just leaving. I love you, too.**

"I'm going to shoot off. Aunt May, do you need a lift?"

"What's the rush? What was the text about?" Debbie asked.

Jolie flushed. *I don't want to lie to them, but they wouldn't understand. They would think I've made a mistake. Have I made a mistake?*

"There's still ten minutes left before we have tae go," May replied, her brow creased.

Jolie swallowed. "I know, but I'm tired, and I have a migraine coming on." *Liar.*

Alec offered to take May home.

Jolie gave Debbie a hug, and promised to come back later that evening. She kissed May on the cheek.

Alec stood, and opened his arms, as he moved forward for an embrace.

She took a deep breath, then forced herself to return the hug.

✳✳✳

Jolie put her key in the lock; soft music seeped out into the corridor.

The scent of roses when she opened the door made her smile.

Dave sat at the table with a bottle of wine and takeaway burgers. "Sorry, but I didn't have time to go shopping and cook something special."

"No, it's perfect."

She sat down, and opened her burger. Dave handed her a glass of wine.

"I can't. I'll be driving later."

His jaw tensed.

Jolie backed up in the chair.

He smiled. "Yeah, sorry I didn't think." He took a bite of his burger.

She stared at the table.

"How's she doing?"

She didn't look up. "Good. They may let her go home tomorrow." Jolie jumped, as he reached for her.

"I'm sorry. I didn't mean to scare you."

His words sounded emotionless to her. *He's not well.* She forced a smile, as she met his eyes. "No, I'm sorry. All the worry with Debbie, and you. I'm on edge.

He winked at her. "Eat up, then we can work that stress off."

***

Jolie slid her legs out from under the covers, perching on the edge of the bed. She rubbed her tired eyes.

Dave's hand stroked her back. "Come back to bed. It's only eight o'clock, and a Sunday morning, the day of rest, woman." He sounded amused.

She stretched her neck. "Debbie's getting out of hospital. I want to pick her up."

His hand moved from her back. "What about the boyfriend?" His tone was harsh.

Not this again. I hate his jealously regarding Debbie. She's my family, my best friend. Jolie peered over her shoulder. "What about him? He isn't her family."

He leaned up on his elbow. "We haven't spent any real time together."

"She's got breast cancer. Please don't be jealous of her; she needs me."

He sat up, and wrapped his arms around her waist. "I know she does, but I'll always want you just to myself."

Dave began nibbling the back of her neck. Jolie squirmed, as his touch sent shivers down her spine.

"Just ten minutes," he mumbled.

"Ten minutes," she agreed.

***

Jolie's eyes sprung open, as her mobile rang. She couldn't believe she had fallen asleep. "Hello."

"Hey, sleepyhead," Debbie said.

"What time is it?" She looked at the clock. "Crap, ten o'clock!"

"The Doctor's just been around, I can go home."

"I'll be there in half an hour." Jolie flung the covers back, and jumped up out of bed.

"No, it's okay, Mum and Alec are here. Pop by the flat later."

Pain stabbed at Jolie's heart. "Alec is taking you home?"

"Yeah. See you later."

"Bye." She put the phone down, and looked at Dave. He was grinning at her. "I wanted to be there."

"You'll see her later. Hey, babe, seeing as you are now up, you could make me a brew." He slapped her backside, and laughed.

She peeked over her shoulder at him. *What have I*

done? This is a mistake. She grabbed her dressing gown, and headed to the kitchen.

Jolie filled the kettle, and switched it on. Spencer darted about in his tank. She leaned on the counter, and traced her index finger on the glass. "I've messed up, Spence. Shit."

Spencer swam to the top of the tank; he looked like he was eating invisible food.

Jolie sighed. "All you care about is your belly. I got you some live brine shrimp yesterday." She picked up the clear plastic bag, and watched the tiny creatures swimming around.

Jolie took the book off the lid. She turned her head, as the kettle clicked off. "It can wait," she whispered, and opened the lid.

She cut the top of the sealed bag away and poured the contents into the fish tank. "Don't eat it all at once."

The china cups clinked against each other when she grabbed them from the cupboard. Steam wafted through the air, as she poured the water into the mug. She heard a plop, turned around, and saw Spencer flying through the air to land on the floor.

"Oh my god." She had left the top off. "Sorry, Spencer." She placed him back in the tank, closed the lid, and positioned the book back on top.

She finished making the drink, picked Dave's cup up, and walked back into the bedroom.

Jolie handed Dave his tea, and sat down on the edge of the bed. Her leg began to shake.

She heard him place his cup on the bedside cabinet. "What's wrong?"

Taking a deep breath, Jolie focussed on her clenched hands. "This…I can't do this."

"Can't do what?" His voice tremored.

"Us." She glanced up at him. "You'll never change."

She looked away when he bent towards her. "I can change. Tell me what you want me to do. I'll do anything." He got off the bed, and got down on his knees in front of her.

Her body tensed when he grabbed her. She forced his hands away.

He edged forward on his knees. "I need you." Tears rolled down his face.

"Debbie needs me. I can't cope with your jealousy, not now."

Fingers stroked her arms. There was a taste of blood on her tongue from biting her lip.

Dark wet patches appeared on the white sheet. "I know you have to spend time with her, I understand that. Please, don't send me away."

She stood up and walked across the room, fear and love fighting the turmoil inside her.

He spun her round to face him.

The cold wall touched her skin, as she backed up.

He turned away from her, and walked back towards the bed. He picked up his cup. Brown liquid splashed up the wall and over the cream carpet, as he smashed the mug on the edge of the cabinet.

Jolie gasped, and closed her eyes. *Oh God.* Her legs felt weak, almost too weak to hold her up.

She heard him shout out.

Blood trickled from his wrist.

"Stop!" she cried out, and ran to his side. Jolie pried the piece of broken china from his hand, and ripped the pillowcase off a pillow. The white material turned red when she wrapped it around his wrist. "Oh god. We need to get to the hospital."

Dave was calm; he stared in her eyes, and shook his head. "No. It doesn't matter. Nothing matters, if I don't have you."

"Please," she begged.

He stroked her face with his bloodied hand. "I love you." He brought the broken piece of china up to his throat.

"No!" She grabbed his arm. "We can try; we can work things out."

His face looked hopeful. "You promise?"

She nodded.

He pulled her into his body, and sobbed into her hair.

Her mind was a jumble; she couldn't concentrate. Images of the film *Carrie*, and blood running down the character's face, brought shivers to her spine. "I'm sorry but I need to look at your wrist, and you're getting blood everywhere."

He let go of her and breathed in a loud shaky breath. "Yeah, sorry."

Jolie led him to the bathroom. She ran cold water over his wounds and wiped them with a cloth. "They're not too deep. Are you sure you don't want to go and get them checked at the hospital?"

Dave shook his head. His face had a surreal peaceful air about it. "There's blood in your hair."

"It doesn't matter. I'll get in the shower in a minute." She patted his wrist dry with a towel. "The bleeding is slowing down."

"I can get in the shower with you, then." He wiggled his eyebrows.

"No, no, you can't." She threw the towel on the floor and opened the bathroom cabinet. "I'm going to bandage this up, and then, you are going to lie down, while I take a shower."

Dave kissed her on top of her head. "I do love you. I didn't mean to scare you."

"I know." She wrapped the bandage around his wrist, and secured it with a safety pin. "Go and rest. I won't be long." She turned away, and switched on the shower.

After Dave closed the door behind him, Jolie slid down to the floor *It's going to be okay. He needs me. I can't let him hurt himself. He loves me, and I love him. This will be good for us both, help mend the past.*

***

Jolie sat at the reception desk, going through the morning's mail. She thought about how good things had been going all week with Dave. He seemed to understand her need to see Debbie. He had food prepared for when she got home from work, and ran her bubble baths every night. He cleaned the flat, and did the washing. He would listen patiently to all her gripes and moans, and hold her when she spoke about her fear of losing Debbie. He made her laugh and smile, and made love to her through the night. She was happy, but a small part of her was scared the old Dave would surface at moment. Her phone beeped with a message from Dave.

Just wanted to tell you I miss you!

She texted back. **I miss you, too. I'll get a pizza on the way back from Debbie's.**

What time will you be home?

Around six. I'm only popping in to see her for half an hour, Jolie replied.

She jumped at the sound of Sophia's voice.

"Will you get coffees ready for when Harold's

client arrives? And not instant!"

"No problem," she replied, with a smile.

Sophia narrowed her eyes at Jolie.

Jolie's phone beeped.

"You've been texting a lot this week." Her brow creased. "You have a new fella?"

"Who has a fella?" Peter asked.

Jolie glanced at him.

"She does. Little Miss Attitude, sitting there, as if butter wouldn't melt. Perhaps now other people can get some attention." Sophia walked between Peter and Jolie. "It's Friday, and I am free tonight."

Peter ignored Sophia, and made his way to the reception desk.

"Who's the lucky guy?"

Jolie thought she saw a look of hurt in his eyes. "I don't want to say, not yet."

Sophia huffed, and walked back to her office.

A forced smile appeared on his lips. "I hope it works out for you. I'm going to the coffee shop, want anything?"

Jolie shook her head, and checked her phone, as Peter walked off.

Can't wait. We can cuddle up on the couch, and watch *The Notebook*.

Jolie giggled. **It's a date, you soppy thing, you.**

***

The sun shone through the open curtains. Jolie closed her eyes to the brightness. She smiled, as she felt his lips on hers. "Morning," she mumbled.

"Good morning, beautiful."

She didn't want to open her eyes, and find this was all a dream. "What time is it?"

He nibbled at her neck. "Nine-thirty. I'm

starving."

She shot up. "Crap. I'm meant to be picking Debbie up at ten."

"She won't mind if you are a little late. You're only going shopping."

Jolie let her mouth fall open, "Only shopping?" She placed her hand on her heart. "Without new shoes, the world as we know it could end. And I've seen some sexy knickers I want."

"Thank god for that." He grinned. "Can I burn the Batman and Minions ones?"

She pouted. "I'm not going to justify that with an answer."

He held his hands up in surrender. "Joking."

She laughed, and slipped on a pair of blue and red Superman knickers, then wiggled her bottom in his face.

He slapped her backside. "Tease. Hey, why don't I come with you?"

Jolie froze.

"I can be ready in five minutes."

Her heart thumped in her chest. "You know, I haven't told anyone about us yet."

His jaw tensed. "Now's as good a time as any."

"No."

She saw a flash of anger in his eyes.

"Why not?" he asked.

She slipped her T-shirt on, and wrapped her arms around him. "I don't want them interfering with us, not yet. You know they won't be happy…after what you did."

"You're right, babe. Let's give it a couple more weeks. Then, we can tell them together."

"Thanks for understanding."

He placed a kiss on her lips, but it lacked emotion. "Will you feed Spencer?"

"Yeah. I'll do it now before I forget," he said dryly, and hauled on his jeans, then left the bedroom.

Jolie finished getting dressed, and put on a little makeup, before joining Dave in the living room. She picked up her leather biker jacket, car keys, and gave Dave a kiss. "I'll only be a couple of hours."

A crease formed on his forehead. "Babe, are you really going out like that?

She looked down at her white sweatshirt, blue jeans, and nude ballet pumps. "What's wrong with it?"

"You haven't got any makeup on."

"I'm wearing mascara and tinted moisturiser."

He scratched his chin. "It doesn't really hide the scars, though, does it?"

She touched the raised lines on her face. "Do you think I should put concealer on?"

"No, no. You look fine."

She bit her thumbnail. "I'll just quickly put a bit of foundation on."

He wrapped his arms around her waist. "Don't be silly." He placed light kisses over her face. "Now, go on. But, don't be long." He squeezed her bottom, before standing back, and opening the door.

Jolie jumped, as the front door slammed behind her. Her head started to ache, and each step vibrated through her body. When she got in her car, she pulled the visor down, and stared at herself. "God, I'm hideous." *I can't stand to look at my face, but I expect everyone else to.* "I'll start making more of an effort." She slammed the visor back up, and started the engine.

CHAPTER 15 BURN BABY BURN

Jolie drooled, as she caressed the white and black leather high heels. "Oh my god. I love these. The fishnet cut-out detailing is gorgeous."

"They're sexy as hell," Debbie said.

Jolie turned the shoe over, and her heart sank when she saw the price on the red soles. "They're five hundred and ninety-five pounds."

"They're Louboutin's, that's not a bad price for his shoes."

Jolie shook her head. "I can't spend almost six hundred quid on a pair of shoes. That would pay this month's mortgage, and still leave enough left over for food." She popped the shoes back down on the shelf.

"I think you should treat yourself." Debbie picked up a pair of thigh-high boots.

Jolie ran her fingers over the tip of the high heels, and then picked up a pair of silver wedges. She sat down, and tried them on. She turned her foot to get a better look, but her eyes wandered back over to the Louboutin's.

Debbie put the boots back on the shelf. "Those silver ones are cute."

Jolie shrugged, and slipped her flats back on. She glanced again at the high heels.

"Would you buy them if they were three hundred?" Debbie asked.

Jolie nodded. "Yeah."

Debbie picked the shoes up, and started to head

for the check out.

"What are you doing?"

"Putting them on my credit card, then you can give me three hundred quid."

Jolie grabbed Debbie's arm. "No, you can't do that. It's too much."

"No, it's not. You never ask for anything; you pay your own way. You are always there for me." A gentle smile crossed her face.

"Without you and Aunt May I would be... I mean, god knows what would have happened to me."

"We love you. And you can consider it an early birthday present. You deserve these more than anyone I know. Your life...I just want you to be happy." The light shone off her watery eyes.

Jolie bought her hand up, and fanned her face. "Stop it, you're going make me cry."

They headed to the check-out, and paid for the shoes. Jolie couldn't stop looking at the bag, as they left the shop.

When they exited the shop, a young man in tight fitting denim jeans walked past. Debbie's mouth fell open, as she stared after him. "That guy's arse is hot."

"What about Alec?"

"I'm just window shopping. It doesn't hurt to check out what's on offer."

Jolie laughed. "Hussy."

Debbie raised her eyebrow. "We can take those shoes back."

Jolie clutched the bag to her chest.

Debbie slipped her arm through Jolie's. "No, that would be too cruel. But, be warned. Vengeance shall be mine." She cackled like a witch.

Jolie held the bag out to her. "Now, I'm scared,

just take them."

A pair of teenage girls glared at them, the corners of their mouths turned down. "Oh my god, I mean, how old are they?"

Jolie and Debbie burst out laughing, and walked into the lingerie shop next door.

Jolie put a black lace bra and knicker set up to her chest, and turned to view herself in the mirror.

"That's pretty, but it's not like you to go for that sort of thing."

"It's... er, I was just looking." She put them back on the rail.

Debbie tutted. "I was joking. If you like them, get them. I love the way my underwear makes me feel sexy."

Jolie picked up the lingerie.

Debbie looked at Jolie from the corner of her eye. "Peter will love the shoes."

"What?"

Debbie shuffled through the bras in front of her. "I remember him commenting on a girl's shoes one night; they were Louboutin's. That guy has an eye for style and beauty."

Jolie sighed. "I know what you're up to, but he doesn't think about me that way. But, he's a friend, and sometimes, I think I care about him more than I should." *Shall I tell her about Dave? No, bad idea.* "I'm happy to have him in my life. I need a friend, more than anything else."

Debbie faced her. "I think he feels more for you than he lets on."

I don't need this, not now. I'm back with Dave. "Can you just drop it?"

A shop assistant approached. "Do you need any

help, ladies?"

"Can I try these on?"

"Certainly, this way."

Jolie followed the woman into the changing room. She slid the curtain across and undressed. The soft lace felt good against her skin. She inspected herself in the mirror, surprised to find a sexy woman, with an hourglass figure, looking back at her. She couldn't take her eyes off herself, as she twisted and turned to see her body from all angles. As she took the lingerie off, she blushed, as she imagined Dave's face watching, as she stood in front of him wearing only her new shoes and underwear. An image of Peter formed in her mind. *Thanks, Debbie. Now, you have me picturing Peter watching me undress.*

"How are you getting on? Do you need any help?" the assistant asked.

Jolie opened the door; she couldn't stop grinning. "I'll take them. Do you have this size in white as well?"

"Yes, I'll wrap them up. Just come to the till when you are ready." She held her hand out for the black set.

Debbie picked up a baby pink basque. "Alec loves me in these."

Jolie watched, as Debbie held it close to her body, and then suddenly burst into tears. A cold shiver ran through Jolie, and she gently took the basque out of Debbie's hand, and embraced her. She bit her lip, and tried to stay in control.

Debbie pulled away, and gave a nervous laugh. "Sorry, I don't know what came over me."

Jolie handed her a hanky. "You're allowed to become emotional. You're going through a hell of a time. I'll pay for my things, then we can go home."

"But, I've only bought a jumper, a pair of sandals, a dress," she looked into her bags, "a blouse, two pairs of jeans, and a play suit."

Jolie brought the back of her hand to her forehead. "The horror. She only has five bags worth of stuff."

As the girls made their way to the car park, Jolie's phone beeped.

How long are you going to be? Dave texted.

Not long, just dropping Debbie off, and maybe stay for a brew with Aunt May. An hour tops, she replied.

"Who was that?" Debbie asked.

Jolie held her breath. *Oh crap.*

A deep crease appeared on Debbie's forehead. "Jolie, you've gone really pale, who was it?"

She turned away from Debbie, and opened the car door. "It was Laz."

"You are not going on another date with him, are you?"

Jolie slid into the car. "No."

Debbie threw her bags on the back seat, as she got in. "What did he want?"

Please stop with the questions. "Just to apologise."

The car's engine purred to life.

"You shouldn't have replied to him; it will only encourage him."

"I wasn't going to blank him, now leave it, will you?" Jolie snapped. *It's not her fault, you're the liar.* "I'm sorry, I didn't mean to snap."

Debbie tilted her head away towards the passenger window. "It's okay. It's none of my business."

The twenty-minute journey dragged with the silence. Jolie pulled up to the kerb outside Debbie's home.

As Debbie got out, Jolie reached over for the bags.

Debbie gave her a weak smile. "Are you coming?"

"Not now, but I'll pop back later."

Debbie walked around to the driver's door, and opened it. "Honey, I'm sorry. I don't want to fight."

Jolie got out, and hugged her. "Me, neither. I'll get us a big fat cream cake for later."

She got back in the car, and drove home. When she got in the flat, she heard Dave's voice coming from the bedroom. When she neared the door, she heard him say, "You know I love you."

Her bags fell to the floor with a thud.

"Jolie," he called out.

A tear snaked down her face.

Dave came out of the room. "Why are you crying?"

"Who were you talking to?"

He glanced to the side. "No one."

Jolie pounded on his chest. "Liar. I heard you, I heard you telling someone you loved them."

He grabbed her in a bear hug. "Stop being so paranoid."

She forced her way out of his arms. "Get out."

His eye went wide.

She sobbed uncontrollably.

"It was my mother, okay?"

Her breath caught in her throat.

"You know what she's like, how she hates me." He slid down the wall, and sat on the floor. "I told her I loved her, and she just swore at me, and told me never to call her again."

Jolie knelt down beside him. "I'm…I'm sorry.

Why didn't you just tell me?"

"Because saying it makes it all the more real."

Jolie put her hand on his shoulder. He shrugged her hand away, stood up, and walked back into the bedroom.

Jolie buried her face in her hands. *First Debbie, now Dave, who else am I going to upset today?* She took a deep breath, grabbed her shopping bags, and made her way to the kitchen.

She plonked the bags down on the counter, and her heart stopped as she spied the fish tanks open lid. "Spencer."

The goldfish lay unmoving on the kitchen floor. "What the hell!" She scooped him up and placed him back in the water. The fish stayed motionless on his side. "Come on little guy."

Spencer twitched, and slowly began to right himself.

Dave walked into the kitchen. "What's all the shouting?"

She couldn't bear to look at him. "You left the lid off. Spencer was on the floor."

His hand banged down on the counter top. "Christ, what am I getting accused of now?!"

Jolie kept her focus on the fish. "I was running late. I asked you to feed to him." She paused. "Were you trying to punish me for going shopping with Debbie?"

His jaw stiffened. "Are you nuts? You think I would try and kill a fish to make you feel bad?"

Jolie folded her arms. "Who else would have left it off?"

"You fed him," he said dryly.

Jolie glared at him. "No, I didn't." She pointed her

index finger at him. "I asked you to do it. You put your jeans on, and said you would do it straight away. I remember it as clear as day."

He visibly relaxed, and took a step towards her. "Babe, your head is all over the place. You did ask me, but then you followed me into the kitchen. I don't think you trusted me. I watched you feed him with my own eyes."

Her brow furrowed, as she tried to remember through the pounding of her head.

"I swear, babe. You have so much on your plate lately. I think you were just on autopilot."

"I don't remember doing it." She rubbed her temples. *He wouldn't do that.*

Dave wrapped his arms around her. "Why would I lie, babe?"

***

Jolie pulled the joint of roast beef from the oven for Sunday dinner.

Dave walked in. "That smells great." He slid his hand around her waist. "The boys will be around to watch the match soon."

"What? When?"

"It starts in fifteen minutes."

Jolie sighed. "I'm just about to serve lunch. You could have warned me you invited people!"

"I told you last night."

She turned to face him. "No, you didn't. And I thought we agreed to not tell anyone about us, just yet?"

"People will find out soon anyway, so what's the difference? And I did tell you last night," he said, as he stroked her cheek. "You are getting so forgetful lately."

She turned away from him.

"It's only the twins. There's enough to go around." He kissed the back of her head.

Her shoulders tensed. "I'll go and see Debbie while you watch the match."

"Good idea. It'll save you from going tonight."

So, I'm only allowed to go once a day? She let out a sigh.

He went over to the fridge. "How much beer do we have?"

How much beer do I have! You haven't paid for a thing since you moved in two weeks ago! She turned the stove off, and picked up the pan of boiling potatoes.

"I'll text the boys to get some more. Can you sub me twenty quid?"

She tipped the pan over the sink, and held on to the lid. "They can buy their own beer, can't they?"

Dave stormed past her, and banged into her shoulder. Her arm jerked, and hot water splashed on her hand and up her arm. She screamed, and dropped the pan.

"What the hell have you done now?" Dave said.

She turned the cold tap on, and let the cooling water sooth the burning. "This was your fault. You banged into me."

He stepped to her side, his face inches from hers. "I get blamed for everything. You step back, and it's my fault!"

Fear coursed through her. She held her breath, unable to think. She tried to stop the tears.

His voice softened, as he said, "I'll get some ice."

Jolie jumped, as the freezer door slammed shut. The ice cracked, as it fell into the tea towel.

Dave handed it to her. "Go sit down. I'll put the lunch out."

Jolie nodded, and left. She gasped when he shouted at her.

"Babe, when you're feeling better, put a touch more make-up on."

***

After lunch was finished, Jolie left for Debbie's.

Her stomach tightened when she looked at her blistering hand hovering over the button for the bell.

Debbie opens the door and laughed. "Good grief. Did you put your make-up on in the dark?"

Jolie nudged passed her. "Very funny."

She sat down on Debbie's couch, the oversized red cushions enveloping her.

"Have you got a new job performing at children's parties?" Debbie's face creased.

Jolie shook her head. "I see you're feeling better."

Debbie put her hand on her hip. "The last time I saw you wearing so much crap on your face you were with him."

Jolie couldn't look her in the eye.

Debbie gasped. "You're back with him." She shook her head. "You've took that two-timing scum back!"

Jolie could feel the anger building up inside, and held her hand up. "That's enough!"

Debbie's eyes went wide. "What the hell happened?" She took hold of Jolie's red and blistered hand.

"I was pouring the boiling water from the potatoes away."

Debbie huffed. "Did *he* do it?"

Jolie pulled her hand away ,and flinched. "Do you really think he would burn me? I'm going home."

Debbie grabbed her arm. "No, wait."

Jolie raised her eyebrows. "What?"

"I have no idea what he's capable of—"

Jolie jumped up.

"Let me finish."

Jolie's ground her teeth together.

Debbie crossed her legs. "I know you think you love him—"

Jolie put her hand on her hip. "I do love him."

Debbie sighed. "If you are happy, then I'm happy for you, but he's a manipulator. You couldn't see it before."

I know she's right, but he's promised things will be different this time. She bit her lip.

"All I'm saying is, question him, question everything."

Jolie sat down. "I'm not going to question him."

Debbie reached over, and took hold of her shoulders. "I'm not being mean; I'm scared for you."

Both their heads turned, as they heard a key go into the lock.

"You better tell her, before she finds out from someone else."

Jolie gulped.

May smiled, as she looked at the girls. "I'm glad yer both here. I have some exciting news…" May frowned. "What the hell happened to yer hand?"

"She can't even boil spuds without hurting herself," Debbie said.

"Have ye put anything on it?" May asked.

Jolie shook her head. "Just ice."

"It looks nasty. I think ye should get it checked out."

"It's not that bad."

"What is it they say? If ye have a blister larger than

a fifty pence piece ye should seek medical treatment," May said, and held her hand out. "Let me see."

Jolie stood up, and let May take hold of her hand.

"The blisters nae quite that size, but yer hand's very red."

Jolie sat back down. "I'll go to the chemist on the high street. I'm sure that's the one open this Sunday. Why don't they just have a regular one, instead of doing these stupid rota things?"

May pointed her index finger at her. "Mind ye do."

"What's the news?" Debbie asked.

May sat down. "They've brought yer dad's parole hearing forward. He could be home before the end of the month."

Debbie and Jolie squealed.

May looked at Debbie. "Where's yer' shadow?"

"Alec was called into work. Jolie has a boyfriend now."

Jolie glared at Debbie.

May gave a little clap. "Sweetheart, that's wonderful, maybe now ye can forget about that deadbeat, Dave. What's yer new man's name?"

Jolie and Debbie looked at each other.

"Deadbeat Dave," Debbie said.

Jolie hung her head when she saw the sorrow – or was it disappointment – in May's eyes.

***

Jolie opened her car door into the street. Out of nowhere, a car horn beeped, and she quickly pulled the door shut again, screaming as a car sped past. She brought her hand up to her mouth, and blew on the raw skin, fluid from the burst blister running down her fingers. Her hand shook in pain.

She made her way up to her apartment, hoping

Dave's friends wouldn't be there. When she unlocked the door, she was met with silence. She closed it with her backside, and lent on it for support. The white paper bag dropped to the floor, as she cradled her injured hand near her chest.

Dave appeared in the hallway, his smile disappearing instantly. "What's happened?"

Her bottom lip trembled.

He picked up the medicine bag, and helped her into the bathroom.

She sucked in air through her teeth, as he gently rinsed the wound and dried the surrounding area, then he put the burn cream onto the gauze, and held it out to Jolie. "I don't want to hurt you."

She closed her eyes. "Just do it."

The cream felt cool on her skin, her hand stung when he pressed the adhesive edge down.

"You still look really pale. You lie down. I'll make you a brew."

She stroked his stubbly chin. "Thanks." She followed him out of the bathroom.

She undressed, and lay on top of the bed, her throbbing hand across her stomach. She sat up when Dave came in. He handed her two pain killers, and her drink. When she took the pills, he took the cup from her, and placed it on the bedside table.

"It tears me apart to see you in pain. I blame myself." He slid in the bed beside her, and buried his face in her chest.

She ran her fingers through his hair. "I know. It was an accident. It was no one's fault."

***

The next morning, Jolie sat at the table in the work's kitchen. Peter passed her, and opened the little white fridge.

With his back to her, he said, "Morning, Jolie. How was your weekend?"

"Morning. It was okay."

Peter sat down, his face stern. "And Dave's?"

Jolie looked away from his intense stare. "How... Debbie?"

"I called around to see her and Alec last night. Why didn't you tell me you were back with him?"

"Because it's nobody else's business."

Peter glanced at her bandaged hand. "So, are you going to tell me what happened?"

"It was an accident, he—"

"What the hell, Jolie?" Peter's chair scraped along the floor, as he leapt up.

Jolie cowered. "It was an accident. I was pouring the hot water away from the potatoes, and he banged into me."

"Then, why are you scared?" He cupped her face in his hand.

I don't know. "I'm always jumpy."

"If I find out he done this on purpose, I'll kill him." All the compassion was gone from his voice.

"Kill who?" Sophia's high heels clip-clopped on the floor, as she sauntered up to the table.

"That arsehole she's back with."

"Dave?" Ridges appeared on Sophia's forehead.

"Yeah, Dave," Peter said.

Sophia breathed in nosily though her nose. Jolie looked up to see the anger in her eyes, and the muscle on the side of her jaw twitch, before she stormed out of the room.

What's her problem? Jolie thought.

Peter barely spoke to her all day, and it hurt her

more than the burn. She couldn't wait to go home, and cuddle up on the sofa with Dave. She daydreamed of eating chocolate, and enjoying the latest Batman film she knew was waiting for her.

She locked the drawer with the petty cash box in it, and grabbed her bag and coat. A scream involuntary left her lips when a hand touched her shoulder.

Her heart pounded in her chest. "Christ, Peter. Make a noise or something next time, will ya?"

"Sorry." He held his arms open for a hug. "I'm sorry about today. It's your life."

She almost threw herself against him. "Today was horrible. Please don't be mad at me again, ever."

His arms tightened around her. She felt safe in his grasp, breathing in his familiar scent. "Promise me you will watch out for yourself."

Jolie felt cold when he let go of her. "Promise." She smiled, and moved towards the door.

"Is Harold back yet?" Peter asked.

She peered over her shoulder. "No, thank god. Sophia had a face like thunder all morning. It was a relief when they left for the meeting."

Peter chuckled. "See you in the morning."

She waved, and left the building. She couldn't stop smiling all the way home. The sound of the shower and Dave singing met her when she entered her apartment. She threw her bag and coat over the chair arm. Dave's phone started ringing.

'Number withheld' came up on screen. She pressed the accept call on the screen

"Why haven't you answered any of my texts?"

Her stomach turned over. "Sophia?"

The phone went dead.

She threw it across the room, and watched it bounce off the wall and land next to the sofa.

She flopped down on the chair. *What the hell would she want with Dave?* She clenched and unclenched her fists. *He wouldn't. Not with her. Would he?*

The shower stopped, and so did his singing.

She picked up the phone and looked in the messages. Empty.

Dave walked into the living room with messy damp hair, and just a towel around his waist.

Jolie held the phone out.

He snatched it out of her hand. "Why do you have my phone?"

"It rang," she said coldly.

His body tensed.

"Why is Sophia calling you?"

His face flushed. "Sophia, who?"

She crossed her arms. "How many Sophias do you know? The one from my work."

His brow creased. "Why would she call me?"

She crossed her arms. "I have no idea; why would she call you?"

"What the hell am I getting accused of now?!" Bits of spittle flew from his mouth.

Jolie huffed.

"You're paranoid!" He stormed off, and slammed the door shut behind himself.

"I didn't imagine the phone ringing, answering it, and a woman asking why you have been ignoring her texts," she shouted after him.

She heard drawers being slammed in the bedroom, and a few minutes later, the living room door burst open and ricocheted off the wall. She jumped at the noise.

"Did they say who it was?"

She stayed silent, the pounding in her chest deafening her.

"Well, did they say who was calling?" he yelled.

She kept her head down. "No, but I recognised her voice."

Dave laughed, and the malice in it terrified her. Her mind went blank, and she just wanted to curl up into a ball and hide.

"You *think* you recognised the voice!" His jaw tense. "I just checked the number. It's my doctor, because I haven't been to see her for a while!" He grabbed her injured hand and shoved her down into the chair.

She yelled out in pain.

"I think you are the one that needs a psychiatrist. You're paranoid." He let go of her, and froze for a second, then knelt down in front of her. "I'm sorry, I forgot about your hand." He wrapped his arms around her.

She sobbed hysterically in his embrace.

"I'm really sorry. I would never hurt you on purpose. It won't happen again." He kissed her wet cheeks.

Her sobbing continued.

His hands cupped the side of her face. "You do know that, don't you? You are everything to me. I wouldn't hurt you, babe. I love you so much."

Jolie stared blankly into his reddened eyes.

He let go of her, and stood up. "You do believe me, don't you?"

His voice sounded distant. She couldn't bring herself to answer.

The door flew open, as he stormed out of the

room.

She shuddered, tried to calm her frayed nerves.

Metal clinked together from the next room. She went to the kitchen to see what was going on.

Dave stood with his arm over the sink, carving knife against the wrist.

She stood in the doorway. "What are you doing?"

"I'd rather die than hurt you. I don't want to have to look at you, and see the pain I caused."

"You need help; you need to sort your anger issues out. If you don't, we won't survive."

The knife clattered in the sink. "I promise I'll see someone, babe."

You better, because I won't do this again. "Okay," she said, and walked away.

CHAPTER 16 THE FOOL

Over the next two weeks, Dave paid extra attention to Jolie. He did all the cleaning, ironing, cooking, and even ran her a bath for when she got home from work. He never grumbled at her for wanting to spend time with Debbie, or going out for a whole Saturday to visit her uncle in prison. Jolie was the happiest she had been for a long while. He played the fool when she needed cheering up, was loving and caring in bed, and comforted her when she worried about her family.

Monday was one of the mornings she needed his strength—Debbie's first chemo session.

Top after top came out of the wardrobe only to end up on the bed, next to half a dozen dresses. Shoes littered the floor.

"Babe, you looked nice in the last ten outfits."

"It needs to be perfect, not nice."

"For sitting in a hospital—"

Her glare cut him off. "If I don't make an effort, she'll know I'm worried. She'll be scared enough, without me adding to it."

"Her mother should be there."

"She didn't expect to be at a funeral."

"Still, she should have chosen her daughter."

Jolie's chest tightened. "Do you really expect Aunt May to miss her own father's funeral?"

"I thought they didn't speak?"

Jolie threw another top on the bed. "He's still her

father, for god's sake."

He kissed her bare shoulder. "Sorry, I'm not helping, I'll leave you to it."

She grunted and continued her search. Finally, she settled for a long-sleeved white tunic top and smart black trousers. She smiled to herself, and picked up the Louboutin's.

***

Jolie knocked on Debbie's front door.

Debbie opened the door. "Morning, honey. Welcome to paradise."

"What's going on?"

"Alec is upset I won't let him come to chemo with us."

Jolie shrugged her shoulders. "I don't mind if he wants to come."

"I don't want him there. You and mum are the only ones I want seeing me like that." Debbie twirled her gold ring around her finger.

Jolie gave her arm a gentle squeeze. "How are you feeling about missing the funeral?"

"I only met him twice. But, he's my grandad, so I guess I should be upset."

"He's, I mean, *was* a stranger." Jolie silently cursed herself for bring the subject up.

Alec appeared behind Debbie. "I can wait in the car?"

She peered over her shoulder. "Alec, I don't know how I'm going to react. I don't want you to see me like that. You can stay here and wait for me."

Alec threw his arms around her.

Debbie hugged him back. "Right, we better go."

They shared a passionate kiss.

As the girls were getting in Jolie's red compact car,

Alec called out, "Call me as soon as it's finished."

"We will," they shouted in unison.

They had been driving on the motorway for about ten minutes, when Debbie suddenly burst into tears.

"What's wrong?"

Debbie didn't answer. She just continued to sob, and Jolie desperately tried to find somewhere to pull over.

"I can't stop. I'll exit at the next junction."

Debbie's torso shuddered, and she said, "No, we'll be late…I'll be ok."

Jolie peeked across at her. "Are you scared?"

Debbie gave a small chuckle in-between the sobs. "It's not that."

Jolie reached over, and gave her leg a squeeze. "Take your time."

Debbie sighed heavily, and settled down. "Sorry, this damn illness is getting to me." She took a tissue out of her bag, and wiped her nose.

Jolie glanced at her from the corner of her eye. "Talk to me. Don't bottle it up."

Debbie flipped the visor down. "I'm okay, really, I have no idea what came over me." She observed herself in the mirror. "Great! Panda eyes."

"There's some wet wipes in the glove box."

The glove box clicked open. "What's this?"

Damn.

Debbie laughed. "Best of the eighties CD. Really?"

"Oh, come on. We grew up to your mum playing that stuff and we all sang along to it."

Debbie popped it in the player. "Karma Chameleon" by Culture Club came on. Debbie covered her ears, as Jolie began to sing.

Jolie playfully slapped her arm.

Debbie winced. "Next!" "The Only Way is Up" by Yazz filled the car.

Debbie turned the volume up. "I love this song."

The girls sang along to the lyrics.

They kept singing along to the CD all the way to the hospital. Jolie laughed, as Debbie chair-danced to the songs, and tried to reach the high notes.

They drove into the car park of the hospital, and the smile on Debbie's face melted Jolie's heart.

Debbie linked Jolie's arm, and they walked into the hospital.

The oncologist nurse showed the cousins into a room, with several large comfy chairs. "We have the room to ourselves for the first hour."

Debbie sat down in one of the blue leather chairs, and Jolie sat in one next to her.

"Do you have any questions before we start?" the nurse asked.

"How soon will my hair fall out?"

A cheerful smile crossed the nurse's face. "We can try and save those gorgeous blonde locks of yours."

"How?"

"With scalp cooling." The nurse picked up a black cap, which resembled a horse-riding helmet, with a hose going into a large grey machine. "For scalp cooling to work, the scalp temperature must be kept low for the whole time the drugs are circulating in the blood. This means the scalp needs to be cold for thirty minutes before the drugs are given, and throughout chemotherapy session, which is one and half hours. Then, we will need to leave it on for about ninety minutes after the treatment has finished." She picked up a chart from the side. "Yep, I have authorisation for it. I'll get you a jug of water, then, we'll get started."

"It's going to be a long morning." Debbie turned to Jolie. "Did you bring the board games?"

The nurse set Debbie up, while Jolie went and got the bag out of the car.

Debbie wrapped the blanket around her shoulders.

Jolie set up the Monopoly board. Before they knew it, the nurse was back with a drip and bag of clear liquid. Jolie turned away, as the nurse stuck the hypodermic in Debbie's chest.

"You and needles. It's over," Debbie said.

When she faced her, Jolie couldn't stop staring at the needle taped to Debbie's chest.

Debbie complained of feeling cold. The nurse brought her another blanket.

They continued their game, then went on to playing card games—snap and gin rummy.

The nurse brought in another woman, who sat opposite the girls, a fancy silver and gold scarf on her head. The woman waved. "Wish I coulda had that," she said, and pointed to the cap. "No good fae ma' cancer." The woman then popped in her ear buds from the MP3 player in her hand, and sat down.

The nurse walked over. "We can take the cannula out now." She looked at the empty plastic bag hanging from the drip.

"I'm going to give Dave a ring—"

Debbie rolled her eyes.

"And," Jolie continued, "get a coffee. Do you want anything?"

Debbie shook her head.

Jolie got a coffee from the cafeteria, and went outside. She sat down on the steps at the main doors, large potted conifer trees guarding each side. She sipped the coffee, and cringed at the bitter taste, then rang Dave's mobile.

"Is that you on your way home, babe?" he enquired.

"No, I'll be a couple of hours yet." She was met with silence. "You still there?" she asked.

"Yeah," he grunted.

"Don't be upset. They're giving her this new treatment, which means she might not lose her hair."

"Great." His tone was flat.

She took a deep breath to try and quell the anger brewing in her gut. "Hair is important to a woman."

He sighed heavily. "Yeah, sorry, babe." His tone still had an edge of anger to it.

"I know you thought we might spend some extra time together, but if I wasn't here, I would have been in work."

"I know. Call me when you are on your way back."

"Okay, bye." She popped the phone in her bag, poured the coffee in the soil, and tossed the cup in the waste bin.

The nurse was sitting next to Debbie when she got back on the ward. She smiled at Jolie, and left.

"Is everything okay?"

Debbie nodded. "She gave me some anti-sickness pills, just in case."

"Do you feel sick?"

"No, I feel alright." She laid the Monopoly board out. "Ready for another thrashing?"

Jolie laughed. "I let you win."

"Yeah, right."

***

Jolie drove Debbie home after the treatment. Alec ran out of the house, before the car had even parked up.

He opened her door. "Are you sure you're okay?"

"I'm fine." She exited and closed the car door.

"I won't come in," Jolie said.

Debbie wrapped her arms around her. "Thanks for being there today."

"Anytime."

***

Jolie went to work the next morning, and for the first time in days, she wasn't worried about how Debbie was. She was confident life was finally coming up roses. She got on with her duties, and even managed to smile at the scowling Sophia. Later that afternoon, the reception phone rang. She was met with the sound of retching, as she said hello.

"Jolie."

Panic stabbed at her heart. "Debbie, is that you?"

Her voice wavered. "I can't stop being sick."

Jolie pulled the phone away from her ear, as another bout of retching took place.

"I took the tablets, but just brought them straight back up again."

"Where's Alec?"

"I was okay when I got up, so he went to work."

Jolie looked at her watch. 3:00pm. "Is Alec on his way?"

"No, he called. I've told him to stay away tonight." She retched again. "I need to lie down."

"Okay, I'll be there as soon as I finish work."

Jolie called Dave.

"Hi babe," he answered, his voice cheerful.

"Debbie's really sick. I'm going around straight from work." She noticed Sophia hovering about out of the corner of her eye.

"What time will you be home?" he asked.

"I'm going to spend the night. She needs looking after, and Aunt May won't be back until tomorrow."

"It's Friday night. Where's her good-for-nothing boyfriend?!"

Jolie flinched, and adjusted the phone. "She's my family, not his." She looked across at Sophia. "I'll call you later."

Sophia placed her hand on the desk, and with a smirk, asked, "You're staying at Debbie's tonight?"

Jolie shot her a 'don't mess with me' look.

The smirk turned into a genuine smile, as she turned away. "Will you tell her I hope she feels better soon?"

Jolie glared after her. *She's sick enough; your name won't make her any better. It would probably make her worse.*

A few minutes later, Harold shuffled into the reception area. "Sophia is concerned; she tells me your cousin is very ill after her cancer treatment."

Gloating, more like. "Yeah, she isn't taking the chemo well at all."

Sophia joined him. Harold grasped her hand and patted the back of it.

Just what's your game, witchy poo?

"Sophia has offered to look after reception, so you can go and take care of her."

Jolie's jaw dropped. "What?" She looked suspiciously at Sophia. "You sure?"

"Of course. I'm not heartless, you know. Now, off you go."

Jolie hesitated for a moment. "Thanks, I owe you one." She grabbed her things, and rushed out of the door.

***

She let herself into Debbie's, and called out her name.

Debbie came into the hallway, supporting herself on the walls. Beads of sweat covered her face, and her hair stuck to her like spiders' legs.

Jolie ran to her, and hooked her shoulder under Debbie's arm, then guided her to the bedroom. She pulled the cover back, and gently eased Debbie into the bed.

Afterwards, Jolie grabbed a bowl from under the kitchen sink, a glass of water, and wet a hand towel.

Debbie tried to sit up when Jolie entered the bedroom.

"Just lie down." She placed the water on the bedside cabinet, and the bowl next to Debbie's arm. She took the towel out, and wiped Debbie's face. "I'm going to call the hospital; I'll be right back."

The hospital told her it was normal, and Debbie should keep taking the anti-sickness pills and drinking plenty of fluids. She would be okay in a day, or two.

Jolie gently cracked the bedroom door. Soft snoring filled the air. She moved the bowl and placed it next to the glass of water, and left Debbie to sleep.

She picked her bag up off the floor, and opened the front door for some air. She sat on the step, and texted Dave.

I'm sorry, but Debbie's in a bad way.

His reply was almost immediate

Doesn't matter, out with the lads anyway.

Thanks for caring. She put the phone back in her bag, and let the door frame take her weight. She jolted, and opened her eyes, as a car door slammed; she couldn't believe she fell asleep on the doorstep.

Jolie peeked in on Debbie, who was still fast asleep. She left two pills in a small plastic cup next to the glass of water, and went for a shower.

After the long hot shower, she heard voices coming from the bedroom. Quickly, she dried herself, wrapped a towel around her wet hair, and popped on Debbie's fluffy dressing gown.

Jolie retightened the robe's belt, and walked in Debbie's room.

Peter sat on the edge of Debbie's bed.

She clung to the edges of the robe. "Peter, what are you doing here?"

He looked her up and down. "Well, hello, sexy."

Jolie's hand automatically went to her face to shield her scars.

"Don't hide that beautiful face from me. I like seeing you without make-up."

She searched his face for any tell-tale signs of his words being a joke.

Nothing. "Are you drunk?"

"What, no. I've just finished work."

Jolie looked down at her pale and washed-out cousin. "How did you get in, Peter?"

"The front door was open."

She looked across at him, her mind a jumble of possibilities for her lack of concentration. Anyone could have come in a robbed them. She shuddered, and closed down the next thought.

Debbie coughed lightly. They both looked at her.

"I'm sorry. How are you feeling?" Jolie asked.

"Like crap."

Jolie looked at the empty plastic container. "You kept the tablets down this time?"

Debbie glared in Peter's direction. "He made me, said you wouldn't have left them, if I didn't have to take them."

Jolie squeezed Peter's shoulder. "Thank you. She

would have been a right pain in the arse with me."

"Sorry, I don't have any energy." Debbie slid down the bed. "I'm just going to close my eyes for five minutes."

Peter made his way out of the room. Jolie tucked the cover up over Debbie's shoulders and followed him.

In the hallway, he asked, "How are you coping?"

"I'm okay."

He took hold of her hand. "If you need anything, just call."

"I don't know what I did to deserve a friend like you, Peter Day. Thank you." She wrapped her arms around his waist. His familiar scent made her feel safe. Her breath caught in her throat. *This is how Dave should make me feel.*

CHAPTER 17 SPENCER

Debbie woke up feeling much better, and when Alec arrived, Jolie went home to get a change of clothes, and see Dave. He hadn't answered his phone, or any of her messages, since he told her he was going out with the lads.

She called his name as she let herself in, and caught a glimpse of him going into the bathroom.

"Dave," she called out again, but he didn't reply. Her stomach knotted up. *Is he still mad at me?* She took a deep breath, and walked towards the bathroom.

The door was open, Dave's arm stretched out above the toilet. In his fingers, orangey-gold scales caught her eye.

"Spencer!" she screamed out, as he opened his fingers, and the goldfish fell.

Jolie ran towards Dave, and screamed as he pressed the flush.

Spencer was gone.

Tears ran down her face. "Why? Why would you do that?" she asked, and pushed him as hard as she could.

He wound her into a hug. "He was dead."

She twisted and turned and tried to get out of his grip. His hold tightened.

"I found him on the floor; he was dead."

She shook her head. "I saw him move, before you let go, he moved."

"He was stiff as a board."

"You killed him."

He tightened his hold even more. Her chest felt compressed; she gasped for air.

"You left the lid off the tank again," he snarled.

"I can't...breathe."

He let go, and chucked her to the floor. A sharp pain made her stomach churn, as her head clunked off the side of the sink. She grabbed the side of her head.

"You left the lid off. He could have been there since yesterday morning, suffocating, gasping for breath. That's a painful death. You're a selfish bitch, who couldn't even be bothered to look after him properly; you were always leaving the lid off."

She brought her hand in front of her face. Blood laced her fingers. "I saw him move," she muttered.

He kicked her foot. "Keep telling yourself that. Blame me, if it makes you feel better. Is that why you are doing this? Well, answer me!"

Her mind went blank. She wanted to hide within herself, never come out again.

"I can't do anything right," he said.

She jumped, as the bathroom door slammed. Sharp pains stabbed at her gut, as she curled up into a ball under the sink, and quietly sobbed. Jolie finally got up, and ran her facecloth under the tap. When the cloth touched her head, she sucked in air through her teeth. She ignored the tapping on the bathroom door.

Dave walked in. "I'm sorry."

She couldn't look at him, and kept her focus on the running water. "You've made me bleed." *In more ways than one.*

He took the cloth from her hand, and gently wiped at the side of her head. "You did this to yourself."

Her shoulders stiffened.

"You broke out of my arms." He lifted up her hair, and kissed her neck. "I should have checked you were okay. I'm sorry."

Get the hell away from me, she wanted to scream, but the fear of what he might do to her, to himself, held her tongue.

"I was so scared you'd find Spencer, I know how much he meant to you, and thought if I could get rid of him, before you got home, you wouldn't blame yourself."

She grabbed the sink, her fingers white. *I don't believe you.*

He kissed her neck again. She felt sick. "I wasn't going to tell you I found him on the floor. That it was your fault."

"Debbie needs me," she whispered.

"And you need me. I'll come with you; help take the burden off you." He let go of her hair. "I reckon this is why your head is messed up, too much worry."

She let out a little squeal of fear, as his hand slapped against her backside.

"No need to try and cope with it all. I'm here."

He switched on the shower, and spun her round and started placing soft kisses along her jaw.

She bit her bottom lip. *Please stop.*

He undid the top button of her shirt.

No, I can't. She trembled with fear. She felt his hot breath on her neck.

He lifted her arms above her head, and took her shirt off.

"Stop," she said, her voice sounded pathetic.

"I love you so much," he said, panting.

"Not now—"

His teeth latched on to her bottom lip. "Yes, now," he said.

His eyes looked wild, her heart thumped in her chest. She didn't have a choice.

***

Jolie unlocked her car, and shuddered at the sound of a male voice behind her.

"Hello, Jolie."

Her body relaxed, as her mind recognised the voice that was somehow different. She turned to face him.

"I'm Bernard Croft."

Jolie smiled, and held out her hand. "Molly's uncle, right?"

He smiled warmly at her.

He looked well, clean. He'd shaved, had on new clothes, his hair had been cut, and he was wearing dentures.

"Get away from her," Dave's voice boomed out.

Fear crossed Bernie's feature, and he visibly coward in front of Dave. "I'm not going to hurt her, don't hit me again, mister."

Images of Bernie falling to the floor at Molly's party, and then an image of Dave's injured knuckles, flashed through her mind.

Dave stepped forward, and shoved Bernie away.

"You beat up an old man?"

Dave yanked the car door open. "He's mental, a nutter, a drunk. Now, let's go."

She watched Bernie limp away, as fast as he could.

"Why did he say, 'don't hit me again'?"

Dave's upper body went rigid, his eyes glared at her.

Fear consumed Jolie.

He stepped forward and stopped, as two men rounded the corner, and threw his arms up in the air. "You know what, just go. I've had enough for one day." He stormed off down the road.

***

Jolie stopped outside Debbie's. She couldn't let go of the steering wheel. Her life was falling apart. Images of Davie's fists hitting Bernie over and over again. A memory she had hidden in the recesses of her mind surfaced.

"How long have you been sleeping with her?"

Dave looked away from her. "Not long."

"Get out. I hate you!"

"I told you it's over," he snapped.

She turned her back on him, so he couldn't see the fear on her face. "Just leave me alone."

"So you can go running into the arms of that idiot, Peter the prick."

"Peter's more of a man than you will ever be," she whispered, and took her phone out of her pocket.

His fist connected with the back of her head, and she flew forward. She threw her hands out to stop herself hitting the wall. The phone landed at her feet.

"See what you've done. Why can't you ever take my side?"

Blood seeped into her mouth, as she bit down on her bottom lip. She had to stay quiet, not scream, not cry, not speak.

"Look at me when I'm talking to you."

She faced him.

"You don't give a damn about me, you never have."

He took a step closer. Jolie gasped. Her phone rang.

"You were trying to call him."

She shook her head.

He grabbed her by the throat.

She let out a scream, and her hand went to her

throat, when a tapping on the window brought her back to the present.

Alec opened the passenger door. "Everything...okay?"

Jolie sunk her teeth into the flesh of her bottom lip. She tried to control her facial features, not show emotion, but knew she had failed miserably.

Alec sat down on the passenger seat.

She leaned away from him.

Through gritted teeth, Alec said, "What did he do to you?"

The muscles in her shoulders tightened.

He reached for her hand. She wrapped her arms around herself.

"Do you want me to get Peter?"

"No," she snapped.

"Okay." He held his hands up.

Relief flooded her.

"Jolie, you are very important to Debbie, and she is very important to me. Which means *you* are important to me." He gave her a weak smile. "Please, let me help you?"

He would kill you. She stared down at her lap. "No one can help me."

"I know I come off as a bit of a joker, but I can look after myself. I want to help. And I don't like him."

"You've never met him."

"I've heard enough. How he bullies you, tries showing you up in public. Last time you were together, he tried cutting you off from your family and friends." He took a deep breath. "He's dangerous."

She held tight to her emotions.

"When someone loves another person with all their heart, they don't hurt them—mentally or physically."

The heat built up in her face. "I know." She sniffed. "He killed my fish this morning. He waited for me to see it happen." She squeezed her eyes shut, and tried to hold back the tears.

In the silence, she could feel the tension in the air. Too afraid not to see his face, she peaked at him from the corner of her eye.

The muscles in his jaw twitched, and his hands were balled into fists.

"Please, don't mention it to anyone. It'll just make things worse."

He relaxed, a little. "Get out. Get out *now*, before he ends up killing you."

Her thumb stroked the faint burn scar on her hand. "He's promised to get help."

"They all do." He reached for her hand.

Jolie held her breath, and moved her hand out of his way.

"Sorry," he said. "He—"

Jolie opened the car door. "Debbie will be wondering what's going on."

Alec joined her on the street. "She's asleep." He placed his hand on her shoulder. "Don't become a statistic."

She nodded, and went inside.

CHAPTER 18 WORRIED

Dave never came home that night. By two the next afternoon, Jolie was worried. She paced around the flat, checking her phone for missed calls or texts. She constantly peered out of the window. *What if he's done something to himself? I couldn't live with that.* She sent a text.

I'm worried about you.

Thought you would have been glad to see the back of me! he replied

I never told you to go. Where are you?

The phone rang. Her heart felt like it was going to burst out of her chest.

"Dave—"

"You can't keep accusing me of things." His tone was stern, but didn't sound as annoyed as she had expected it to be.

"I know. I'm sorry." Her shoulders dipped.

"I still need to clear my head. I'll be home later."

The phone went dead. She looked at it in her trembling hand. *I don't know if I want you to come home.*

Jolie lay awake, as sleep evaded her. She checked the time again. Midnight. The front door clicked shut. She turned over, and wrapped the cover tight around her face. The bedroom door creaked. Dave stumbled about, and banged into the door, then the wall, before his shoes dropped to the floor. His clothes rustled, as he took them off. She held her breath. The mattress dipped and bounced, as he slid in beside her.

He snuggled up to her, and looped his hand around her waist. "Are you awake?"

She stayed silent. His boozed-filled breath snaked its way up her nostrils. Soon, his snoring filled the room. Jolie still didn't dare move. Eventually, sleep took hold of her.

***

When Jolie woke, the sun streamed in the bedroom through a gap in the fluttering curtains. Dave grunted, and heaved the cover over his head. She didn't want to wake him, and slowly slid out of the bed, careful not to tug on the covers. The drawers squealed when she opened them. She held her breath, and peeked over at Dave. He didn't move. After she had showered and dressed, she went to feed Spencer. Her fingers grabbed the food, and her stomach knotted up. *He's no longer here.*

The silence was deafening. No talking to her fish, no rumbling of the kettle for her coffee. She grabbed her bag and keys, and slammed the front door shut behind herself.

She expected a phone call from Dave, as she drove to work, complaining she had woke him up. Calling her names. But, she didn't care. She would tell him how she felt; she was sure she would.

The call never came.

Jolie stood with her back against the red brick wall behind the reception desk. Her fingers explored the uneven texture, but even this did not ease the tension in her body, or mind.

Peter walked past, said good morning, and rushed off into the kitchen, not waiting for her to reply.

What's wrong with him? Panic rushed through her. *Alec's told him.*

She followed him.

Sophia sat at the table munching on some biscuits.

"Peter, can I have a word?" Jolie asked.

Sophia got up, and Peter glared after her, as she left.

"Not now, Jo, I'm in a bit of a rush." His eyes never met hers.

A pain stabbed at her heart. "Okay, maybe later."

"Sure." He walked out, and still never made eye contact.

What have I done? The reception phone rang. She walked back to her desk, and answered it.

"Good morning! McCarthy, Richards, and Day. How may I help you?"

Peter slipped his jacket on, and walked out the front door, never acknowledging her.

Why's he acting like this?

Jolie watched the door all day, waiting for Peter to return. Eventually, Harold locked the doors, and Jolie made her way to her car feeling hurt, confused and alone.

When she arrived home, she wanted to wrap her arms around Dave. Have him tell her that he loved her, and everything was going to be okay. Deep down, she knew Dave wasn't perfect, but he loved her, and he would be there to comfort her. That beat going home to an empty apartment any day.

The noise was first thing that hit her, a female voice shouting, "Harder, harder, yeah, yeah, oh god…." She held her nose, as the smell of stale beer and smoke hit her.

Dave lay on the couch in just his boxer shorts, beer cans littered the floor, an over-flowing ashtray on the side table.

She switched the TV off.

He grinned at her. "Babe, you're home," he slurred.

She glared at him. "What's going on?"

He patted the cushion next to him. "Come sit down."

"Look at the state of the place. Who's been smoking in here?"

"Stop moaning."

"Stop moaning? The place is like a pigsty. It stinks, and you're watching porn."

Dave jumped up, grabbed her arms, and slammed her into the wall. Her stomach wrenched, and she screamed out. His fingers dug into her flesh.

"You're hurting me."

He let go, and stepped back.

Jolie's knees buckled, and she slumped to the floor.

"I'm sorry. What have I done?" Dave knelt down beside her. "I didn't mean it." He clutched her to his chest. "I swear it will never happen again."

The hairs on her body stood on end, but her mind was blank, closed off to the world and its brutal reality.

Back and forth, he rocked her in his arms.

Jolie had no idea how long she had stayed in his rocking embrace. But, eventually, he was snoring loudly. Inch by inch, she slid out from him. He woke when she stood. She froze.

"Babe." His brow creased, and his eyes lingered on her arms. He pointed at her bicep. "I didn't mean…"

She looked down at the deep bruising at the top of her left arm. Then, across at the right one, three small but nasty looking bruises above her wrist. *I've been a fool, believing you.*

She gasped, as he grabbed her hand.

"Please don't leave me. I promise I'll never do anything like that again—" His words meant nothing, she was numb. "I might as well end it now," he continued.

Jolie snatched her hand away, and walked out of the room. He called out after her. She ignored him, and closed the bathroom door behind her.

When she emerged after a long soak in the bath, Dave had cleaned up the flat.

"I've made your favourite, chicken and bacon salad," he said.

His eyes pleaded for forgiveness, but she wouldn't meet them.

"I'm not hungry." She stared at the empty fish tank. "Get rid of that," she said, no emotions showing. "I'm going to bed."

***

Jolie flipped the page of her book, as the bedroom door opened. She peeked up at Dave. Gone was the anger, replaced by pale features, and somehow, he seemed smaller.

"Can I come in?"

Jolie closed her book. "What do you want?"

He made his way over to her, shoulders slumped, eyes focussed on the floor. The bed dipped when he sat down.

"I promise I'll never hurt you again."

"You've said that before." She picked up her book, and began reading.

"I'll get help?"

"And you've said that before, too." She put the book down, and met his gaze. "When did you last see your doctor? And I don't mean GP. When did you see your psychiatrist?"

He looked down at his lap, guilt written all over his face.

She sat up straighter. "I want to come to the next appointment. When is it?"

"It...it's not allowed," he stuttered. "I can ask if you can come the next time I go."

She faced away from him on her side. "I won't be coming home tomorrow night." She sensed him stare at her back. "I'm going to Debbie's. Actually, I'll probably be eating with her every night this week."

"Why don't you invite her over here?"

Jolie shot him a look. *What the hell are you playing at?*

"I want to be more involved with your family, and make an effort to get to know them more, and her new boyfriend. We might become mates." He shrugged. "You never know."

She flipped herself over. "Do you mean it?"

He stroked the side of her cheek. "For you, yeah, I'll try."

***

Jolie wore her long sleeve, baby blue shirt to work, to hide the ugly purple and blue bruising on her arms.

Peter stood at reception. "Hi."

"Hi yourself. You going to talk to me today?"

His cheeks turned a slight shade of pink. "Sorry."

"What was going on? I thought I had really upset you." She reached over for the pile of post. Her sleeve slid up her arm.

Peter took hold of her wrist. "What the hell happened?" he demanded.

Jolie pulled her arm back. "Nothing."

His face contorted. "You don't get bruises for nothing."

"Dave—"

He slammed his hand down on the desk. Jolie jumped back.

"What the hell?"

"If you would let me finish." She glared at him. "He was teaching me self-defence. He didn't hurt me on purpose." She couldn't maintain eye contact with him.

Peter's eyes narrowed. "Really?"

He knows I'm lying. Her face flushed. "Yes, really."

Peter huffed, and walked away.

"I'm sorry," she whispered, and sucked her bottom lip in to her mouth.

Jolie didn't see anything of Peter for the rest of the day, or the next day, or the day after that. Before she knew it, Thursday had come, and it was time for Debbie's chemo. This time, Aunt May went with Debbie. Jolie headed straight to Debbie's from work.

Debbie looked well, just a little tired, and wanted to sleep. They promised to call Jolie, if anything happened. When she got home, Dave was in a grumpy mood, and wouldn't speak.

She tried to keep herself occupied by cleaning, then reading, then cleaning the kitchen again. When bedtime finally arrived, sleep evaded her. She tossed and turned, until she finally fell asleep on the couch around one in the morning.

CHAPTER 19 PAROLE

Jolie arrived at work fifteen minutes late on Friday morning. She yawned, as she saw the pile of mail waiting for her. Then, she stopped when she spied a chocolate heart on her desk with a note.

Sorry, I'm an idiot. Forgive me?

She picked up the chocolate heart, and opened the clear packaging.

"Bit early for that, don't you think?" Peter said.

She chuckled. "So, we both have faults. You're an idiot, and I eat chocolate before nine in the morning." She scowled at him. "Where've you been?"

"I took that job in Inverness, for McTaggart's. The company wants to commission us to do their refurbishments." He sauntered past. "I have to go. We'll speak later."

Jolie nodded, and the phone rang. She picked it up. "Jones, McCarthy, and Day."

"Good morning sweetheart, ye have a brammer telephone voice."

She went rigid. "Aunt May, is everything alright? Debbie-"

"Now, now, calm yerself. She's fine. But, I do have news."

Jolie smiled into the phone. "Uncle Mike?"

"Aye, Mike got his parole; he'll be home on Friday."

Jolie squealed with delight. "Oh my god. That's terrific. I'm…oh my god."

"I'm going to have a wee party for him, if ye must, bring that low life with you."

Jolie rolled her eyes. "Aunt May."

"Aye, aye, ye love him. I canna say yer uncle will take kindly tae him."

She shuffled about on her chair. "He'll be on his best behaviour, I promise. How's Debbie?"

"She's fine. Nae being sick, nothing. I have to go. Bye, sweetheart."

"Tell Debbie to call me on my lunch. Bye."

"Nae bother, sweetheart."

Jolie could not stop smiling throughout the morning, even when Sophia walked past, and said she looked like she should be licking windows.

Jolie went to the bakers at the end of the street, and got a cheese sandwich and a cola, then walked over to the park and sat on a bench to enjoy her food on the unusually warm autumn day. She had just popped the last of the sandwich in her mouth, as the phone rang.

"Debbie, how you feeling?"

"Great, no problems with sickness, just a little tired."

A breezed ruffled Jolie's hair, and she shivered. "Great news about your dad."

"Isn't it amazing? We'll have to get him something for his homecoming."

Jolie wrapped her cardigan around her. "That's a great idea. What you going to get him?"

"Not sure yet. Mum's going to take me shopping later. I'll text you."

Jolie briskly rubbed her arms. "Great. It's getting cold here, so I'm going to head back in work."

"Okay, I'll text later. Love you."

"Love you, too." Jolie put the phone away, grabbed her rubbish, and half-jogged, half-walked back to work.

Jolie thought about calling Dave and telling the good news, but she feared he was probably still going to be in a mood, and she didn't want him to spoil the day for herself.

***

Jolie had just gotten home when her phone beeped.

"Who's that?" Dave said. He eyed her suspiciously

"It'll be Debbie. Uncle Mike's coming home on Friday. There's going to be a party for him." She smiled. "You can get to know all the family better, like you said."

Dave grunted.

Jolie got her phone out.

I got Dad a cockring

Jolie burst out laughing and replied, **No!**

No, a cockring, Debbie replied.

Jolie giggled again. **I'm going be a little bit more conservative, and get him a new jumper.**

Dave peered over her shoulder.

OMG, I can't stop laughing. I got him a J o e C o c k e r CD.

Phew, I was worried there for a moment, Jolie replied.

"What's so funny?" Dave asked.

Jolie showed him all the messages.

Dave huffed. "Typical of the way her mind works, She'll never change."

"What do you mean by that?"

"Nothing." His eyes burned with anger.

A cold tremor went down her spine. She took deep breath to calm her nerves. *He's not well.*

All week, Jolie was on pins. She secretly hoped Dave wouldn't want to go the party, but Friday came, and he was in a better mood, claiming to be looking forward to meeting Mike.

Jolie's legs shook, as she sat on the sofa, waiting for Dave to finish getting ready. She smoothed over the wrapped parcel. *What if he hates Dave?*

Dave coughed from the doorway, getting her attention. He looked handsome in his dark blue denim jeans, torso hugging polo shirt, and grey wool jacket.

"You scrub up pretty well, Mr. Green."

He held is hand out, and as she stood, he surveyed her 1950s style rockabilly red dress. "Damn, woman. You are one sexy lady."

Jolie giggled.

He locked his fingers in hers. "Let's go and meet the infamous Uncle Mike."

"Please don't wind Debbie up. That will just annoy him."

"When she gets a load of this—" He waved his hand down in front of himself. "She will be putty in my hands."

Jolie huffed. "Somehow I doubt that."

"Relax, it'll be fine."

Jolie heart pounded in her chest, as she pressed Aunt May's doorbell. The door opened, and there stood her uncle.

His greying hair was cut short. His cheeks touched the bottom of his gold framed glasses, as he smiled at her.

Jolie let go of Dave's hand, and flung herself at Mike. "I still can't believe you are actually home."

He sniffed loudly, and she swallowed the lump in

her throat.

He gently stepped out of her hug. "I've missed you guys." He peered over her shoulder at Dave.

"This is Dave," she said.

Dave held out his hand, and frowned, as Mike took hold of it in his. "Good grip there, Mike."

"Prison does that to you," Mike replied.

Jolie stepped between them. "Shall we go inside?"

Mike smiled at her, put his hand on her back, and led her inside.

Aunt May gave her a hug, and said 'hello' to Dave.

The living room was cramped, as they had set the table up at the far end. The two comfy chairs were jutted up next to the sofa.

Debbie gave Jolie a kiss on the cheek, then took the gift from her, and handed it to Mike.

Dave walked up to Jolie, and wrapped an arm around her waist. "Hello, Debbie."

"Hiya," Debbie said, and turned away. She held the gift out. "Open it, Dad."

Mike took the parcel from her.

"Where's Alec?" Jolie asked.

"He's gone to pick Peter up."

Dave tightened his hold on Jolie. She could feel the tension radiating from him.

Debbie smirked. "Dad insisted Peter should be here, because of how good a friend he's been to us all."

"The kitchen looks great," Mike said. "And nice of Peter to pay for the cabinets. I remember him as a kid. He always had a snotty nose. And a smile on his face, despite his home life."

The doorbell went again, and then, Peter and Alec walked into the living room.

Peter gave Jolie a weak smile, before glaring at Dave.

"Peter, you look well lad," Mike said, and pulled him into a hug.

Dave's fingers dug into her hip.

Alec waved at Jolie, and she waved back.

"Food's ready. Now, take a seat everyone," May said.

Dave kept his grip on Jolie, as they all turned to face May.

"I'll give you a hand, Aunt May," Jolie said.

May waved her off. "Nonsense. Sit down. It's under control."

Debbie, Alec, and Peter had already sat down. Mike sat at the head of the table, and patted the seat to his left.

Jolie hesitated, as she realised Dave would be sat opposite Peter.

Mike smiled at her. "I get to have my two favourite girls next to me."

Jolie sat down, and Dave rubbed her thigh. She blushed at looked around to see if anyone had noticed. They didn't appear to have.

May served up the food, and then sat at the other end. Everyone chatted among themselves, at the same time, tucking into a meal of steak, potatoes, peas, and carrots.

Dave kept touching Jolie's hair. Now and then, he placed a kiss on her cheek or her shoulder.

Mike and Peter glared at him ,and Jolie wriggled about, as she felt uncomfortable.

"Dave, please. We're eating," she whispered. "What's wrong with you?"

"Nothing, I'm fine." He looked across at Peter.

"Just showing my girl some love."

Peter's eyes narrowed.

"Who wants chocolate cake?" May asked.

Everyone said they would like a piece. Aunt May brought the cake in, and Debbie went and got dishes for everyone.

Jolie started collecting the empty plates, and Alec helped her. While she was rinsing them off at the sink, Alec joined her.

"I don't like him. He's not right for you," Alec said.

Jolie glared at him. "You don't know him." She turned the tap off.

"He's treating you like you're a possession."

"He's got a controlling nature, but he's good to me, not that it's any of your business." She put the plug in the sink, and switched the tap back on.

"When was the last time he was good to you?"

Jolie scanned her mind, as she poured the washing up liquid into the sink. She couldn't think of one time when what he did didn't benefit himself, somehow.

Alec gave her arm a gentle squeeze.

Jolie stared at the bubbles, as she slid the plate in the sink.

"Come on. Let's grab some of that cake before it's all gone."

She shook her head, and followed him back into the living room.

Mike had got the whiskey out, and Dave sat there with a face like thunder, holding a large glass.

"Having fun?" Dave said, as Jolie took her seat.

"Just rinsing of the dishes."

Mike offered her a whiskey.

She shook her head. "I'm driving."

Everyone relaxed, and filled Mike in on the latest gossip on the small estate; what pubs had closed and the new shops which had opened up. Apart from Debbie and Jolie, they all seemed to be getting a little tipsy.

"Oooh, Mike, get out the cigars I got from my trip abroad," May said.

Debbie and Jolie cleared the table, and Mike, May, and Dave went to the garden to smoke.

"I didn't know Dave smoked." Debbie said.

Jolie peered over her shoulder at him. "Apparently, he does when he drinks."

Peter and Alec folded the leaves of the table in, and carried it into the kitchen.

"Coming out to the garden?" Debbie asked.

"In a minute," Jolie replied.

As Debbie went out, Jolie walked towards the kitchen, she froze, as she heard the conversation between Peter and Alec.

"It's too much seeing her with him, the way he treats her. I'm handing my notice in on Monday, they only need a month's notice," Peter said.

"You have to tell her, don't just leave. She needs you."

No, you can't leave. The pain tugged at her heart, and realisation slapped her in the face. *Oh god, I'm in love with him.* Her eyes began to water.

Moments later, and in a more composed state, Jolie walked into the kitchen. "You're leaving?" Her voice betrayed her, cracking slightly. She coughed to disguise it. Alec left the room, without saying a word.

"Things are complicated." Peter walked closer. "You need to leave him."

Give me a reason. She bit her bottom lip.

"He doesn't deserve you."

She gasped, as Dave appeared at her side.

"And you do?" Dave snarled.

"You're a bully," Peter growled.

Dave squared up to Peter.

"Stop it!" Jolie shouted, as Mike walked in the kitchen.

"What's going on?" Mike glared at Dave.

"Nothing," Jolie said. "We're just leaving."

"Jolie," Peter called out.

"Leave it, please."

She grabbed Mike's arm. "I'll see you tomorrow. Tell Aunt May and Debbie I said goodbye."

***

Jolie tried to open her eyes, but she just didn't have the strength. The slow constant pounding in the back of her head was growing with every breath. Her shoulders hurt and so did her stomach.

Why was she still in the living room? She moaned in pain when she tried to get up.

Memories started flooding back. Dave had hit her, more than once.

She could piece together parts of their argument; it was about her spending too much time with Alec and Peter, especially Peter.

How long had she been out? Attempting to open her eyes, the left one wouldn't move. "Shit." She cautiously examined it with her fingers.

Vast waves of pain flooded down her right cheek, and her shoulders quaked.

She grabbed her phone, and tried to text Peter, the letters were blurred, and she barely found his name. She kept it short.

Come get me.

A text pinged back. She refocussed, and just made out the words.

I'm on my way.

She gasped, as Dave grabbed the phone. "Who are you calling?"

"No one." Tears bounced on the edge of her trembling lips.

"And here come the water works again."

She hugged herself. "These are the last tears I'll ever shed because of you. I want you to leave."

He grabbed her hair, and forced her head back. "So you can have him? You've been sleeping with him, haven't you?"

"It's nothing to do with him. It's you."

He let go of her hair, and paced the room. Then, he stopped by the window. "What's he doing here?"

Jolie saw her opportunity, and ran for the front door. She threw it open, and took the stairs running. Her heart hammered in her chest, as she heard him following her, screaming, and calling her a whore.

She opened the main door to the street, and banged straight into a man. She flipped over, and landed on her side. Dave ran towards her. Bernie blocked her view.

"Leave the girl alone," he said to Dave.

Dave chest-bumped him.

"Go on, hit me again. I don't care. But, you are not getting near her."

Dave laughed. "Daddy to the rescue."

Her mind tried to process what Dave had said.

The sound of screeching tires filled the air.

"Jolie, I have to go now," Bernie said. "He's gone. You're safe now."

"Who are you? What do you want with me?"

"Another time," he said, and walked away from her.

"Jesus, what did he do to you?" Peter said.

Sirens sounded in the distance. She held her arms out to him. "Peter."

Two police officers were at her side, before she realised they were for her. One of the officers grimaced, as he looked at her, and radioed for an ambulance. The officer asked her questions, and she told them what had happened.

Peter closed his eyes. The muscles on the side of his jaw rippled.

An ambulance blared up behind the police car.

When the paramedics approached, the police moved to the side, taking Peter with them. Peter kept peering over his shoulder at her.

The paramedics insisted she go for an x-ray. They were worried her eye socket was fractured.

***

The X-ray results were good, and no bones were broken. She was given painkillers, and information on concussion. Peter insisted she wasn't to go back to her place, that she should stay with him, on the off-chance Dave would come back. Jolie wasn't afraid to go home; she was more afraid of seeing her family. She made Peter promise not to say anything, and told him, despite his concerns, she was going home. He was more than welcome to stay with her.

Peter grabbed some things from his house, then drove Jolie to her flat.

Her hands shook so much, she couldn't get the key to fit in the door. Peter took hold of her hand, gently took the key from her, and opened the door.

She stood in the living room. There was blood

on the chair nearest her—her blood. The side table lay smashed on the floor. In the carpet, shards of glass sparkled like diamonds, as the winter sun shone through the window. She jumped when Peter touched her arms.

"Why don't you go and have a soak in the bath? I'll clean up."

Jolie was grateful to leave the living room, and lay down in the warm water, bubbles encasing her, the smell of vanilla and coconut filling the room. Her emotions went wild. She silently cried, as the anger, sadness, fear, then finally relief flooded through her. She was free. She picked her phone. Time to call the family.

Debbie, May, Mike, and even Alec had wanted to come around. Mike and Alec said they were going to comb the streets looking for him. But, she heard Aunt May in the background, warning Mike about his parole conditions. Jolie persuaded them to stay away; she was safe with Peter. And she promised to see them the next day.

With the towel wrapped around her hair, and the bathrobe closed tightly around her torso, she allowed herself to peer in the mirror. Her eye was almost closed with the swelling. Black, blue, purple, and green coloured it. She pointed at her reflection. "Never again." She spun to the door, when she heard the sound of something being dragged down the corridor.

As she opened it, Peter was dragging two large black bin bags to the front door.

"Hey," he said, and smiled brightly at her.

"Hey," she replied. "What's that?"

"His stuff. Just going to drop in it the bin." He opened the front door. "Lock it behind me." Then, he was away, dragging the bags behind him.

She ran to the door, and put the chain on. *Shit, he'll go mad.* She giggled. "Serves you right, David Green." She almost skipped into the living room.

There wasn't a trace of broken furniture, or blood, anywhere. *How long was I in the bath?*

A knock came from the front door. "It's me," Peter said.

When she opened the door, it felt right, having Peter there. She smiled at him.

He raised an eyebrow at her. "What are you up to?" he said, and closed the door behind himself.

"Nothing," she laughed. "I can't even smile at my knight in shining armour now?"

Peter frowned. "I did nothing; he was already gone by the time I got there. If I find him—"

"Stop, please, for me."

"Okay." She remembered about Bernie, and what Dave had said to him. "'Daddy to the rescue,'" she said out loud, as she sat down on the couch.

Peter sat next to her. "What?"

"That's what Dave said to Bernie. Bernie stood up to Dave. He said something about he didn't care if Dave hit him again, but he wasn't going to hit me. And Dave said, 'Daddy to the rescue.'"

"Why would he say that?"

Jolie shook her head, removing the towel. "I have no idea." She ran her fingers through her hair.

"Let's not worry about that now. You need food and painkillers."

"I couldn't eat anything."

"Just a bit of soup." He nudged her. "For me."

After they had eaten, Jolie looked out of the window. "It's snowing," she said. "I love the snow. Can we go for a walk to the park?"

Peter readily agreed.

Jolie dried her hair and dressed.

***

The park was quiet, hardly a soul about, apart from the odd dog walker. Jolie cuddled into Peter's side, and he laced his fingers through her gloved ones.

"I love it here when it's snowed. Everything is so clean and fresh," she said.

When they got to the centre of the park, Peter wiped the snow off the old wooden bench, and they sat watching the squirrels foraging. The weak winter sunshine forced itself through the grey clouds, determined to be seen. Like the sun, she felt it was now her time to shine.

"Promise me something," he said.

"Anything."

"You will always be part of my life."

She wrapped her arm around him "Always."

A gang of rowdy teenagers throwing muddy snowballs at each other stopped not far from them.

"Wish I was that young again," Jolie said.

"Come on, old woman, let's go and get a brew. I'm freezing. These old bones can't take the cold like they used to."

Jolie giggled. "Okay, old man. Can we come back later, when it's a bit darker? It's feels quite magical in the right light."

Peter cocked his head to the side. "I didn't know you were a romantic?"

"It's sad, really. I've only ever sat here by myself when it's snowed at night."

"Then it's a date."

They made their way back to the flat. When they got inside, Peter got the quilt and a pillow out of the bedroom, and made Jolie comfy. He put a film on. When he sat down beside her, Jolie leaned into his chest.

Jolie spent half the time hiding under the cover as they watched *Thirteen Ghosts*. Although, she fell asleep halfway through.

She woke up, as the front door closed. Frantically, she looked around the living room. Empty. "Peter."

He popped his head around the door. "You're awake."

"Who was at the door?"

"Just me. Get your coat on," he said.

Jolie looked confused. "Where are we going?"

"To that magical land in the centre of the park."

***

The snow had stopped, and as they neared the centre, Jolie could see tiny flickering lights. The closer she got, the more detail she made out. It looked like dozens of candles in glass holders.

Peter stopped walking,

She looked at him. "What's going on?" she asked.

"If you sit at the bench, you can see the message."

Jolie walked up to the bench. I LUV U was spelled out in three-foot lettering, made by the gentle sway of the candles. Tears blurred her vision. She put her hands over her trembling mouth. "You mean it?"

He nodded. "With all my heart."

Jolie held her breath, as Peter placed his hand around her waist. She almost died when he drew her in close, staring down into her eyes. Her whole body began to tingle, and her heart pounded so loud, she thought the world would hear it.

He glanced at her lips, as he bit his own, and then, looked back into her eyes. He cupped her face with his right hand, and slowly started to lean his head forward.

Jolie closed her eyes, as his warm soft lips connected with hers. She wrapped her arms around his neck, and kissed him back.

This isn't the end, it's just the beginning.

I hope you enjoyed the story, but if you have been affected by any of the issues in the story these are a

few websites you may find helpful.

UK

http://napac.org.uk

USA

http://www.pandys.org/crisissupport.html

http://www.pomc.com/survivors.html

ABOUT THE AUTHOR

British born, DM Wolfenden is a horror addict, and grew up reading Stephen King, Dean Koontz and James Herbert. To this day, they remain some of her favourite authors. She also use to watch a lot of the old, British Hammer House of Horrors. She has a fondness for animals and tattoos. Whilst a bit on the shy side, she works in a mostly male environment. A radio operator on a semi-submersible oil rig in the North Sea.

DM is always happy to interact with readers, you can contact her on any of the below social media sites.

Twitter: @dmwbhbe

Facebook: @DMWolfenden

Printed in Great Britain
by Amazon